To Do

Meeting with Jackson 2 p.m.

Cancel Thurs. handball—don't reschedule

Pick up dry cleaning

Buy diapers!

Find a NANNY ASAP!!!!

Please address questions and book requests to: Harlequin Reader Service
U.S.: 3010 Walden Ave., P.O. Box 1325, Buffalo, NY 14269
CAN.: P.O. Box 609, Fort Erie, Ont. L2A 5X3

Born in the USA

HAWAII

BARBARA BRETTON

Daddy's Girl

Harlequin Books

TORONTO • NEW YORK • LONDON
AMSTERDAM • PARIS • SYDNEY • HAMBURG
STOCKHOLM • ATHENS • TOKYO • MILAN
MADRID • WARSAW • BUDAPEST • AUCKLAND

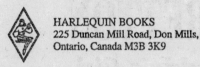

HARLEQUIN BOOKS
225 Duncan Mill Road, Don Mills,
Ontario, Canada M3B 3K9

ISBN 0-373-47161-0

DADDY'S GIRL

This edition published by arrangement with Harlequin Books S.A.

® and TM are trademarks of the publisher. Trademarks indicated with
® are registered in the United States Patent and Trademark Office, the
Canadian Trade Marks Office and in other countries.

Printed in U.S.A.

Dear Reader,

Any man can be a father, but it takes a special man to be a daddy.

That old saying was true when I was growing up, safe and secure in a traditional nuclear family of the 1950s, and it seems to me that **it** still holds true today in the 1990s. Fatherhood is a **bio**logical fact. Daddy-hood, however, is something much more difficult to define.

Daddy warms up the formula, lets Mom sleep in on Saturdays, and changes diapers without being asked. Daddy is there to cheer every Little League home run, and somehow never sees the strikeouts that came before. Daddy knows which dragons to slay…and which ones you have to slay yourself.

Hunter Phillips had no interest in fatherhood. Babies were mysterious aliens who inhabited a milky world of Pablum and car seats and pediatricians. When Daisy, his late sister's newborn baby girl, comes into his life he finds his entire world turned upside down. He'd never failed at anything before, but, then again, he'd never figured on fatherhood.

Is reluctant father Hunter Phillips daddy material? I guess you'll just have to read *Daddy's Girl* and find out!

I'd love to hear from you.

Barbara Bretton
P.O. Box 482
Belle Mead NJ 08502

With love to my father,
RTF & F

Prologue

Hunter Phillips had sky-dived over the Arizona desert, faced a hungry shark off the Mexican coast and skied *off-piste* in Klosters, but he'd never known fear like this.

For three weeks he'd scraped by on neighborly advice, emergency room visits, and how-to tapes from the local video store, but now he was stumped.

"Don't cry," he said to the squalling infant in his arms. "There's nothing to cry about."

She was dry. She was well fed. She was warm. As far as he knew, that about covered all the bases. Babies didn't worry about deficit spending or nuclear disarmament. The videotape he'd rented last night said newborns had simple needs and those needs could be simply met.

So much for modern parenting.

"Come on, Daisy," he said, pacing up and down the length of his apartment. "I'm as new to this as you are. Give me a hint...a clue...anything."

Daisy screwed up that tiny face of hers and yowled even louder.

"I'm impressed," he said, wincing. She had amazing lung power but he'd settle for just one declarative sentence. Or half of a sentence. One word that would help him find a way to stop her crying.

Hunter had never been able to cope with a female's tears. When the female in question was blond, blue-eyed and weighed a little over six pounds, the issue became even more unnerving.

Everything about Daisy was terrifying. That soft spot at the top of her head…the tiny bowed legs…the knotted umbilical cord that only a few short weeks ago had been her lifeline. The first time he'd held her he'd felt huge and clumsy, a bear trying to hold a butterfly in his paw. His gut still knotted each time he picked her up, but at least he could manage it now without feeling she was about to slip through his fingers.

But this crying was something else. She sounded as if she had the worries of the world on her fragile shoulders. Her wails tore at him. No matter how hard he tried, he couldn't understand what she was trying to say. As far as he was concerned, Daisy might as well be from another planet.

"I don't like this any more than you do, Daisy," he told the infant. He wasn't cut out for fatherhood. This wasn't supposed to have happened. He'd been going along with his life, minding his own business, and pow! Suddenly there she was, a tiny scrap of humanity all alone in the world except for him.

Daisy deserved better. She deserved a real family with people who loved and wanted her. She sure as hell didn't deserve a single-minded advertising executive who'd only stop and smell the roses if there was a sixty-second TV spot involved.

He touched her forehead with the back of his hand. She seemed cool but who was he to judge? It was only two o'clock in the afternoon. The pediatrician would be in the office. Maybe he'd call for a radio cab and take Daisy over to see the doctor.

"Okay, Daisy," he said, wrapping her up against the late September chill. "If you won't tell me what's wrong, maybe you'll tell the doctor." She'd better tell someone and fast, because Hunter was at the end of his rope. No one and nothing had ever made him feel as helpless as Daisy did just by crying.

The radio car was waiting outside at the curb. A slender black woman who was somewhere in her fifties leaned over to open the door.

"Fifty-fourth and Third," he said, buckling Daisy into the car seat he'd lugged downstairs. Daisy's wails sounded even louder in the confines of the car.

"Poor little thing," said the driver as she pulled out into traffic. "Is she sick?"

Hunter shrugged. "I don't know. She's been crying like this for two hours. Something's got to be wrong."

"She's a baby," said the driver with a chuckle. "Comes with the territory."

"Nobody'd cry like this if there wasn't a problem."

"Maybe she felt like a ride around town."

Hunter snorted. "Give me a break," he said.

The driver chuckled again. "She's not crying anymore, is she?"

He sat up straight and stared at Daisy. "You're right. She's quiet." Not only quiet, but falling asleep.

"Happens all the time," said the driver. "I raised three of them myself and I can tell you I don't know what parents did before God invented cars." She stopped for a red light. "Still want Third and Fifty-fourth?"

"No," he said. "Let's just drive."

She smiled at him through the rearview mirror. "Smart man."

No, he thought, as they headed for Riverside Drive. A smart man would never have gotten himself into this mess in the first place.

Chapter One

"Where's the kid?" bellowed the director, a neurotic Yale graduate with quadruple ulcers. "You can't expect the model to work without the kid."

Hunter Phillips had a pretty good idea how Custer must have felt at the Little Big Horn. "Where's the kid?" he asked the production assistant standing next to him. "This is a diaper commercial. You can't do a diaper commercial without a kid."

The assistant's eyes widened as she looked at Hunter. "I thought that was the kid."

"This is *my* kid," he said, switching eight-month-old Daisy from his left shoulder to his right. "Where's the pro?"

The assistant clutched her clipboard close to her chest and took a deep breath. "I don't know."

"What's going on, Phillips?" The director looked as if he was on the verge of ulcer number five. "Time's money."

You learn that in Yale? Hunter wondered. "Denise

went to check it out. You know traffic. They're probably stuck in the Midtown Tunnel.''

The producer cast an appraising eye on Daisy. ''How about her?''

Daisy chose that moment to spit up apple juice on the jacket of Hunter's last surviving Armani jacket. It was the end of an era.

''Forget I said anything,'' muttered the producer. ''We need a pro.''

''Damn right,'' muttered Hunter right back. No way was Daisy going to be dragged into this circus just because somebody somewhere screwed up. Casting had hired Amanda Bennett, the country's top toddler model, for the spot. Only thing was, Amanda was nowhere to be seen and you damn well couldn't shoot a high-profile thirty-second spot for biodegradable disposable diapers without someone who wore the things.

The young production assistant hung up the wall phone and turned to face the assembled employees of Crosse, Venner and Saldana, advertising agency to the stars. ''The mother's changed her mind,'' she said, her eyes brimming with tears. ''She signed the kid up exclusive with Pampers. We're out of luck.''

All eyes turned toward Hunter and Daisy. ''Forget it,'' he said. ''She's camera shy.'' Advertising people were born opportunists. He should know. He was one.

''It's fate,'' said the casting director. ''Karma. You have to let us test her. If we don't give the old man something by five o'clock our collective ass is grass.''

Talk about being between a rock and a hard place.

Daisy had awakened six times last night and Hunter was running on an hour's sleep. That might have been enough at twenty-two, but at thirty-four, it wasn't even close. Only 10:00 a.m. and already his brains were fried.

The big boss at C V & S wasn't very enthusiastic about providing day care while Hunter struggled to find someone to help out with Daisy. Through the years he'd heard a lot of talk about day care and nannies, but he'd never paid much attention to any of it. You had a kid, you took care of it or you found someone else to do the job while you went about your business. He'd quickly learned otherwise. Looking at Daisy, he felt that rush of emotions that still took him by surprise. How did you leave someone so small and helpless alone with a stranger?

Unfortunately he hadn't been able to convince the powers-that-be to look into the needs of the other parents on board at C V & S. They'd made it painfully clear that they were bending the rules for him on a temporary basis and anything less than total fealty on his part would be grounds for a pink slip.

Hunter was ambitious. He considered it one of his finer traits. These days, however, he was finding it tough to balance ambition with responsibility.

If he refused to be a team player in this minicrisis, there was a better-than-even chance he'd find himself out on the street with his laptop computer and his little girl.

"Give me a couple minutes," he said, heading for the door. "I'll grab my Rolodex and see what I can do.'' He wasn't about to hand over his daughter without a fight.

Pushing open the swinging door, he stepped out into the hallway and found himself face-to-face with a gorgeous model. She was leaning against a wooden ladder and smoking a cigarette with her gaze trained on him like a laser beam. She was one of those tall and curvy blondes who made a living by selling people things they didn't want. Back in the old days when he had a libido, she was the kind of woman who had a major effect on him.

Hunter grinned. The goddess smiled back. It had been a while since he'd flirted with anybody. New fathers didn't have a lot of time for flirting.

''Hi,'' she said.

''Hi,'' he said, pitching his own voice somewhere between Rambo and a caveman.

''You're all wet.''

''What?'' He'd heard some weird opening gambits in his day but this was in a class by itself.

She glanced down and then away. ''Your trousers. You're all wet.''

He groaned, visions of a romantic interlude vanishing as Daisy gurgled happily and tugged at his ear with chubby fingers. The model drifted back into the studio, leaving him standing there with egg on his face, apple juice on his shoulder, and the usual all over his pants. There was nothing like reality in the form of a soggy diaper to bring a man back down to earth.

''Thanks, Daisy,'' he muttered to the rosy, fair-haired baby with the cornflower-blue eyes. "You have something against leggy blondes?"

"She wasn't your type."

He blinked. Up until now Daisy hadn't uttered a word. This would be one hell of a beginning.

"Up here," said the breezy female voice. "On the ladder."

He looked up and saw a small figure clad in black leggings and a bright red sweater. A white T-shirt peeked through the low V-neckline and a huge pair of shiny gold hoops dangled from her ears. She was perched on the top rung of the ladder.

"Forget the Vogue model types," she said blithely with a toss of her short cap of sleek black hair. "They never know what to do in an emergency."

"And I suppose you do?"

"Club soda. It can work wonders."

"I'll keep that in mind."

"I wouldn't wait too long if I were you. Once that stain sets, you're done for."

"Look," he said, growing exasperated, "I appreciate the advice, but I have more important things on my mind than washing out stains."

"I know," she said in a wry tone of voice. "She *was* great-looking but she went back inside."

"Forget Marcy," he said. "I'm looking for someone younger."

"Better be careful," she said over her shoulder as she climbed down the ladder. "You can get in trouble that way."

"A baby," he said, shifting Daisy back to the original shoulder. "You don't happen to know where I can find one, do you?"

"So it's true," she said, looking up at him with light blue eyes the same color as Daisy's. "I'd heard a rumor that Amanda's gone over to the competition."

"Took her training pants and ran." He gave her a second look. "Are you with Fancy Pants Diapers?"

"I'm the baby wrangler."

His eyes widened. "The what?"

"The baby wrangler," she repeated, laughing.

He entertained a bizarre image of the woman tussling with an infant. "What's a baby wrangler?"

"I'm the one who coaxes all those adorable smiles out of them for the camera."

"You're the miracle worker," he said, grinning. "Why didn't you say so the first time?"

"Not much point," she said in her breezy way. "Without the baby, I'm nothing."

"Same here. If I don't dig up a replacement pronto, I'll be pounding the pavement."

She stepped closer and he caught the scent of fresh flowers as she took Daisy's little hand in hers. "She's beautiful." Her eyes met his. "I think she'd be a natural."

"No way," he said. "Find yourself another baby to wrangle."

"Look, Mr...." She paused.

"Hunter."

"Look, Mr. Hunter, I—"

"Hunter's my first name."

Daisy blew bubbles from her perfect little mouth and both Hunter and the woman laughed out loud.

"Jeannie Ross." She extended her hand. Her grip was firm. Her hand was soft.

"Hunter Phillips."

"There's nothing in it for me, Hunter. I get paid whether we shoot or not."

Daisy stretched her chubby arms toward Jeannie.

"What is this?" Hunter asked. "A conspiracy?"

"May I?" Jeannie reached for Daisy and the baby went to her eagerly. "She's beautiful."

Hunter noted the easy way Jeannie held Daisy—and the look of bliss on his daughter's face as her chubby hands tugged at the shiny earring.

"I don't want my kid in show business."

"One photo shoot does not a career make," Jeannie Ross pointed out. "Besides, what choice do you have? If you don't find someone soon, you're history. You said so yourself."

He winced. "Are you always this blunt?"

Her smile softened her words. "I find it saves time."

"One hour," he said. "If they can't get a decent shot in sixty minutes, she's out of here."

"Agreed." She looked at Hunter and shook her head. "Now relax, will you? You have my word she'll have a wonderful time. I'll see to it."

As a rule Jeannie made a point of spending time with her young charge before shooting began, but the director quickly nixed that idea.

"No time," he said, with another glance at his fancy watch. "We've wrapped the prelim shots and another account is coming in at two." He eyed Daisy, whose chubby arms were wrapped around Jeannie's neck. "I hope the talent's up to it."

Jeannie smiled brightly through her annoyance. "She's a natural," she said in her most optimistic tone of voice. "I guarantee you'll be pleased with her."

He muttered something ominous and glared over at Hunter, then walked away.

"That does it," said Hunter. "If that son of a—"

"I agree," said Jeannie, "but he won't get anywhere near Daisy." She nuzzled her face against the baby's neck. "She's all mine."

She explained to Hunter that the rules and regulations involved in using babies on the set were clearly laid out and Jeannie made certain they were rigorously adhered to.

"Technically I'm here to keep things moving along, but there's more to shooting a good commercial than making a baby laugh on cue."

"It's crying I'm worried about," Hunter said. "I know these people and they'd work Mother Teresa into the ground if it meant making an extra dollar."

"Look," said Jeannie, drawing him aside. "You need this account badly, don't you?"

He nodded, a forbidding scowl on his face.

"Then let me handle this. If it isn't right for Daisy, I'll stop things immediately."

"I believe you," he said, the scowl lessening. "Damned if I know why, but I do."

They stood there for a moment—man, woman, and child—and Jeannie experienced the oddest sense of destiny.

Ridiculous, she thought, excusing herself and Daisy and heading into the fray. It was only business. Nothing more.

But there was something different about the situation, something she couldn't explain, that made her feel as if this was only the beginning....

"Oh, thank God! Thank God!" The young production assistant, clutching her ever-present stopwatch, raced up to Jeannie and her young charge. "Time's money! If we don't get some baby footage soon my head is going to roll."

It occurred to Jeannie that at least ten people had already claimed that their futures rested on Daisy's tiny shoulders. She suspected that only Hunter Phillips was telling the absolute truth.

She smiled at the production assistant. "Now let me see if we've got the setup straight. The model picks Daisy up, walks with her to the window, then—?"

"Tight shot on the kid. She gives us a big toothless grin—you know the kind, the ones without spit bubbles—and it's a wrap."

"Got it," said Jeannie. "Come on, sweetie," she whispered in Daisy's ear. "Let's show him how to do it."

THE USUAL CROWD was there.

The anxious director gulping Maalox between takes. The young production assistant timing each scene with Swiss watch precision—and all-American enthusiasm. A mustachioed makeup artist who seemed more interested in the blond model's boobs than her blusher. Camera people, sound operators, gaffers, grips, and a bored-looking set nurse playing solitaire in the corner.

Hunter had never paid much attention to the mix before, but today it occurred to him that he'd never seen a more obnoxious group in his life.

The thought of his little girl being placed in their grubby hands made his guts twist. If it weren't for Jeannie Ross, he would've grabbed Daisy and headed straight to the unemployment office.

Daisy wailed once when the assistant put the slate in front of her and dropped the clapstick to mark the start of Take 1. Jeannie was there in an instant, soothing the little girl and making sure no one put the slate in front of her face ever again.

He watched the proceedings with a mixture of dismay and pride as the baby girl breezed through the taping with a minimum of fuss. Even the director, as hard-bitten as they came, couldn't keep from grinning at Daisy's charm.

Hunter was surprised at the pang he felt as he watched his little girl getting along fine without him, but once he did, Hunter found himself noticing that Jeannie was not only good to look at, but she was a natural herself when it came to dealing with the inarticulate demands of a baby. Crouching on the sidelines, she made funny faces, blew soap bubbles, and did anything it took to keep Daisy smiling and happy.

Maybe there really was something to the notion of "maternal instincts" after all, because even after eight months, he still had trouble translating some of Daisy's cues.

Poor kid. Even a stranger understood the baby better than he did. Jeannie didn't ask for anything Daisy couldn't easily and naturally deliver and she even ran interference between the little girl and the director.

"She's the best in the business," whispered the young production assistant as Jeannie coaxed Daisy to laugh for the camera.

"Daisy?"

The assistant shook her head. "Jeannie. I'll bet she could work every day of the week if she wanted to."

Hunter didn't disagree. Babies were big business these days. Everyone from Madison Avenue execs to Hollywood hotshots were clamoring for toddlers to sell their wares. Jeannie was one of the select few who knew how to turn screaming toddlers into seasoned pros.

According to the assistant next to him, the commercials Jeannie had worked on had won numerous CLIO awards—and generated income for the ad company involved. The two movies she'd been involved with were box office smashes, with special kudos for Jeannie's work with the babies who were integral to the stories.

"She's so good with kids," murmured the assistant. "What a shame she doesn't have any of her own."

He glanced toward her ring finger and noted that it was bare. Not that it was any of his business whether or not she was married. Still it surprised him that she was unattached.

There was a warmth about her, a tenderness, combined with a subtle sexuality that struck him as more potent than the blatant appeal of some of the models he'd dated in the past. The fact that her petite frame was perfectly proportioned didn't hurt, either.

Just as Jeannie had promised, Daisy's work was over before the hour was up. Hunter found he was almost disappointed.

"The kid's great, Phillips," said the director after he called it a wrap. "Could get herself a lot of work if you're willing."

"Forget it," said Hunter, scowling. "This was her first and last appearance."

"Your loss," said the director. "Not many kids that age with so much personality."

Jeannie Ross approached Hunter with Daisy straddling the curve of her hip. "Your daughter is a dream," she said with a smile that made her blue eyes twinkle. "I almost wish the shoot had taken longer."

Hunter reached for his daughter who started to cry when Jeannie handed her over. "At least her timing is good," he said over Daisy's wails. "She waited until she was offstage."

Jeannie patted the baby's bottom. "I think you have a little problem here."

He grimaced. There were some aspects of fatherhood that he hadn't quite come to terms with yet. "Maybe I should ask for payment in Fancy Pants Diapers."

"They don't stay babies forever," she said. Her voice was bright but the twinkle in her eyes seemed subdued. "Enjoy her while you can."

He shifted Daisy to his other arm. "You did a great job this morning. I'm impressed."

She dipped her head in acknowledgment. "Thanks. Some women are rocket scientists, others are baby wranglers."

"I've heard you're one of the best in the business."

"Small business," she said. "Not a great deal of competition."

"You should learn how to take a compliment, Ross. I don't hand them out often."

"Then tell your boss," she said brightly. "I can always use the work." The twinkle was back in her blue eyes. "But tell him that as of tonight I'm on vacation." She had one more assignment this afternoon and then she was free for the next six weeks, after which she flew to the island of Maui for a job.

"Why don't I get Daisy's diaper situation squared away, then maybe we could grab a bite to eat somewhere. I owe you for saving my butt back there."

She hesitated, her gaze resting on Daisy. "It isn't that I don't appreciate the offer, Hunter, but I don't think I—"

"No problem," he broke in. Obviously Daisy was

the real attraction here. "Thanks again for taking such good care of her during the shoot."

She gave the baby's foot an affectionate squeeze. "My pleasure. She's a doll."

Daisy let loose with another wail of distress and Hunter felt instantly guilty. "I'd better change her."

Jeannie nodded. "See you around Madison Avenue, Hunter."

He watched as she disappeared down the corridor. "So much for flirtation," he said to Daisy as they headed back toward his office where he'd stashed the diaper bag. There'd been a time when women had actually sought his company. These days it seemed as if Daisy was the only female eager to spend time with him.

Not too many of the women he knew were itching to jump into a ready-made family. Having a baby was one thing; raising someone else's baby was another thing entirely. That was one thing he knew firsthand.

His last date had been over five months ago and there wasn't another one anywhere on the horizon. Which was probably a good thing since he barely had time to brush his teeth in the morning, much less manage a social life.

"She wasn't my type anyway," he said as he headed down the hallway toward his office. He liked tall, leggy blondes. Jeannie Ross scarcely topped five feet, if she was lucky and her hair was as black as a starless sky.

Still he had the oddest sense that they had only just begun....

ONCE IN HIS OFFICE, he shoved aside the fax machine and a portable car seat, and changed Daisy on the credenza, right next to a stack of million-dollar ad presentations waiting to be signed off on. Hard to believe there'd been a time when his office had looked like an office and not a branch of Baby World.

"Ingenious use of company furniture," said a dry male voice from the doorway.

Hunter, diaper in hand, glanced over his shoulder. Walter Grantham, the boss of bosses at C V & S, offered up one of his executioner's smiles. Daisy, oblivious to danger, happily kicked her chubby legs in the air.

Hunter ditched the dirty diaper in the garbage pail and reached for a clean one.

"What can I do for you, Walt?" he asked Grantham as he slid the fresh diaper under Daisy's bottom. No point in stopping the proceedings now. Not even Hunter was clever enough to pretend he was doing anything but the obvious.

"Good going," said Grantham, aiming his smile at Daisy. It was the first time he'd looked at the baby as anything other than a pain in the butt. "You pulled our fat out of the fire. Team spirit. That's what we need around here…more team spirit."

"We'll have to fill out forms on Daisy." Hunter fastened the diaper securely then rummaged through the diaper bag for a pair of pink ruffled pants. "Social security card, all that sort of thing. The government's pretty clear on the requirements." *And so am I.* He damn well expected his daughter to be paid for her labors. Daisy might not command the same fee as the talented little Amanda, but his daughter was no slouch.

"Of course, of course," said Grantham, although Hunter could see that the notion of compensation had taken the man by surprise. "Personnel will see to everything." Again that killer smile. "We have to keep our young star happy, don't we?"

Hunter quickly glanced around for the guillotine in the corner or the firing squad hidden behind the drapes. He scooped Daisy up in his arms, then leaned against the edge of the desk. Grantham, of course, remained standing. Everyone at the ad company had majored in intimidation in school—Hunter, included. Trouble was, you could only look just so intimidating with an eight-month-old baby sucking on your silk tie.

"Hunter," said Grantham, "we need to talk...."

JEANNIE WAS STANDING on line at the deli that evening when she saw him. At first she wasn't entirely sure that the exhausted-looking man with the baby girl asleep on his shoulder was the same sophisticated ad exec she'd bantered with earlier that day, but that rough-hewn profile of his was a dead giveaway. You didn't see too many men in the middle of New York City who looked as if they'd ridden straight out of a Marlboro commercial. He was leaning against the other end of the long counter, his eyes at half-mast, apparently waiting for his order to be prepared.

"The usual, Jeannie?" Tuna-on-rye-hold-the-mayo, extra pickles, and a Diet Pepsi.

"And a brownie. It's been a long day."

Al shook his head. "Believe me, I like your business, Jeannie, but when're you going to make yourself a hot meal?"

"Oh, you know how it is, Al," she said, stealing another glance at Hunter Phillips who seemed to be asleep on his feet. "Never enough time to get to the supermarket before it closes." Not entirely forthcoming, but true enough.

As far as Jeannie was concerned, there was no lonelier place on earth than the express checkout line on a weekday evening. You could tell a lot about a person by peeking into her grocery cart. Those cans of soup-for-one were a dead giveaway.

Al set about putting together her order. Jeannie turned slightly and glanced at Hunter for the third time in as many minutes. The sight of that beautiful blond baby nestled in his arms brought a lump to her throat. If men had any idea how effective it was on softhearted women, bachelors would rent babies and stand around looking ruggedly vulnerable.

So go say hello, Jeannie.

She hesitated. She'd only met him once and that had been strictly business.

You know you loved that baby. Wouldn't it be nice to hold her in your arms one more time?

She took a step back. All the more reason to stay away. The last thing she needed was to get attached to his little girl, even for an instant.

Take a good look at him, Jeannie. He's a pathetic sight.

Gorgeous dark-haired men with muscles to spare couldn't be pathetic if they tried. He probably had an equally gorgeous wife at home and three more adorable children.

"Here's your sandwich, Jeannie." Al leaned across the counter and handed her a brown paper bag. *"Bon appétit."*

"See you tomorrow, Al." Taking the bag, she started for the cash register, certain she could make her getaway without being spotted by Hunter Phillips.

She was about to pocket her change and vanish when it happened.

"Jeannie? That's you, isn't it?"

Slowly she turned around. "Hunter." She gently touched the sleeping baby's foot. "Hi, Daisy."

He looked even more exhausted up close. Dark circles ringed his beautiful hazel-green eyes and he stifled a yawn. His fancy silk tie looked as if it had been caught in a threshing machine and his slacks had never recovered from the accident that morning.

Strangely enough, none of it mattered. The truth was, the man looked more splendid tired and rumpled than most other men looked on their wedding day.

"You live around here?" he said, shifting Daisy's position.

Jeannie nodded, trying hard not to notice the way the baby's chubby hand rested against her daddy's cheek. "The old prewar building across the street."

He whistled low. "I know that place. High ceilings, great view...how'd you manage it?"

"Dumb luck. I came to town just as my old college roommate was leaving. I'm subletting." *Okay, Jeannie. The ball's in your court.* "Are we neighbors?"

He gave her an address two blocks away. "Not as impressive as your building, but we like it."

We. Hunter and Daisy? Hunter and wife and Daisy? *Just ask, you fool. It's not against the law.*

"Pastrami on rye, extra mustard, side of slaw," called out one of the counter clerks.

"Over here," Hunter said. "I'll be right with you."

"Look," said Jeannie, "I don't want to keep you from your dinner."

He started fumbling around for his wallet, trying to balance briefcase, diaper bag, and sleeping child.

"Let me help you," said Jeannie. She reached for the briefcase and diaper bag. He handed her the baby instead.

Daisy's cornflower-blue eyes fluttered open. She gave Jeannie one of those unfocused, sleepy looks that children specialized in, then popped her thumb into her mouth and promptly went back to sleep. For a moment she was tempted to hand Daisy over to the cashier and run for her life, but reason intervened.

You work with babies eight hours a day. Hugging them, playing with them, wiping away their tears. This isn't anything different.

But it was. Jeannie didn't know how or why, but from the first moment she saw Daisy and Hunter, she'd had the feeling that life would never be the same.

"Ridiculous," she said out loud, nuzzling Daisy's sweet-smelling neck. She was tired and hungry and not thinking clearly. A baby was a baby was a baby. Tomorrow she'd be working with Amanda or Troy and Daisy would be another chubby little face in her scrapbook. "What's taking your daddy so long?" She glanced toward the counter where Hunter was engrossed in conversation with Al. Hunter held a brown paper bag like her own and was about to take possession of another bag twice its size.

"You have quite an appetite," she remarked when he approached.

"This is mine," he said, lifting the smaller of the two bags. "The other is for both of us."

Her mouth dropped open in surprise. "For the both of us?"

"Yeah," said Hunter as if they'd been through it a hundred times before. "I wanted to take you to lunch this afternoon."

"And I said no." She tried to ignore the fact that Daisy's face was now pressed against her cheek. "I never mix business with pleasure."

"We're not doing business anymore. Daisy is retired."

"Perhaps," said Jeannie, "but you aren't."

"Don't worry. The odds of us working together again are a million to one." He rarely handled advertising accounts that had anything to do with children or pets. She never handled anything else.

"How do you know I don't have a husband at home waiting for me?"

The expression on his face told her he hadn't remotely considered his invitation in a romantic light. "He's welcome to join us." He paused a beat. "*Are* you married?"

She shook her head. "Are *you?*"

"No. It's just Daisy and me."

He had the kind of smile a woman felt in body parts she hadn't realized she possessed. Not that it mattered to Jeannie. She was no more interested in him that way than he was interested in her.

"So what do you say, Jeannie? Just dinner. No strings attached. The place is a pigsty, but I can clear a spot for us at the table easy enough."

She thought of her own immaculate apartment. Quiet. Pristine. *Lonely.*

"Why don't you and Daisy come to my place?" The words were out before she realized what she was doing.

"Sounds great." He traded his bags of food for his baby daughter. "Let me drop my gear off at home and grab something for Daisy and we'll be over."

"Ring twice and I'll buzz you in," she said. "The doorman's on vacation."

"Half an hour?" Hunter asked.

She nodded. "Perfect."

Chapter Two

"So what do you think?" Hunter asked as he buttoned Daisy into the red-and-white sweater his office assistant had knitted for her. It was early May and the evenings were still cool. "Is this a date or isn't it?"

Daisy happily waved her chubby legs in the air then blew a spit bubble.

"That's about what I thought," said Hunter. "It's not a date."

So this was what it had come down to: asking an eight-month-old baby for advice on his love life.

"What love life?" he said, scooping up Daisy into his arms. His once energetic social calendar had disappeared somewhere between Daisy's birth and the introduction of solid foods.

No wonder he'd entertained a fleeting glimmer of hope that Jeannie Ross's impromptu invitation was something more than a humanitarian gesture.

"We must've looked pretty pathetic in the deli," he said as he grabbed his leather jacket and slung it over his shoulder. Daisy'd been asleep in his arms and he'd practically been out on his feet himself.

But not anymore.

He gathered the rest of her paraphernalia. Funny how meeting up with a beautiful and sympathetic woman could put the wind back in your sails.

"Okay, Daisy, here are the ground rules," he said as they rode the elevator down to the lobby. "No food fights, no spitting up on your hostess, and no cussing. Got it?"

"Daah," said Daisy.

Got it.

TWENTY MINUTES later Jeannie wasn't so sure this was a good idea.

The apartment was in the same immaculate condition in which she'd left it that morning, but still she raced from room to room, dusting, polishing, and making sure everything was in order. When you lived alone, it was easy to keep the place clean, but Jeannie couldn't resist making doubly certain things were in order. It wasn't every day she invited a total stranger home for dinner. God only knew what had possessed her to ask Hunter and Daisy to her apartment, but ask them she had.

When Jeannie had moved in, Clare had said that Jeannie could make any changes she wished, but she had been content to leave things pretty much as is. She'd added a few Ansel Adams prints and a pair of ivory rugs that had set her back a month's salary and that was it.

The English country decor begged for family photos scattered here and there, but she didn't need framed snapshots to make the memories any more clear than they already were.

"Enough of that," she said out loud, heading into the kitchen. She refused to live in the past. Besides, Hunter and Daisy would be there in less than five minutes and the table wasn't even set. Working quickly, she found her favorite taxicab-yellow plates on the top shelf, the ruby glasses in the cabinet over the refrigerator, and her best flatware in a shoebox tucked away in her bedroom closet.

Jeannie couldn't remember the last time she'd set a proper table. Mostly she met her friends in local restaurants or cafés for a quick bite and the latest gossip. There was something eminently satisfying about arranging plates and napkins and silverware in the proper pattern and knowing there would be someone other than yourself to enjoy it. More often than not, Jeannie ate in front of the television, watching game shows or sitcom reruns.

"Daisy!" She stood in the middle of the dining area with her hands on her hips. She didn't have a high chair or a booster seat. None of the paraphernalia babies required. Maybe she should call information and get Hunter's telephone number and—

Too late.

The doorbell rang once, then twice.

Jeannie's heart did a little jig inside her chest. "You don't get out enough, lady," she muttered as she checked her reflection in the mirror one last time. This wasn't a date with Mel Gibson, for heaven's sake. She was splitting a pastrami on rye with a bachelor father from the ad agency and his adorable little girl.

It wasn't a date.

It wasn't even the beginning of a beautiful friendship.

It was just a sandwich and nothing more.

IT TOOK HER A WHILE to open the door. Hunter and Daisy waited patiently while Jeannie undid the various locks, chains, and bolts city life demanded.

"Hi," she said as the door opened wide. "Come on in."

"How'd you know who it was?" he asked, sounding uncharacteristically protective. "You didn't look through the peephole."

She laughed and ushered him inside, then closed the door behind him. "You rang twice, remember?"

"Anyone could ring twice. That's not exactly a secret code."

"You surprise me, Hunter," she said, holding out her arms for Daisy. "I wouldn't have figured you for a worrier."

"Try eight months of instant parenthood," he said as he put Daisy in her arms.

She looked as if she wanted to say something but thought better of it. "The coat closet's to the left of the door," she said.

He shrugged out of his battered leather jacket, one of the few items of clothing Daisy had yet to mark as her own. "It's okay. I'll drape it over a chair."

"Did you bring Daisy's things?"

He gestured toward a large canvas bag at his feet. "Everything short of her night-light."

Jeannie handled the baby with the ease of someone who'd had a great deal of practice. Hunter was frankly envious of the casual way she balanced Daisy on one hip while she rummaged through the bag. Before he knew it, Jeannie had spread a blanket on the floor next to the dining room table, right on top of a fancy hand-knotted carpet. Strange, but Daisy's brightly colored toys looked right at home.

And so did Daisy. Jeannie didn't blink an eye when the baby scooted across the blanket and onto the expensive rug, blowing spit bubbles as she went.

"Don't worry about it," Jeannie said when Hunter dived to retrieve his peripatetic daughter. "The rug's mine, not Clare's, and it's survived worse than Daisy."

There was nothing about her warm and open manner to belie her words. Babies came with certain built-in drawbacks. Wet diapers. Spit-up. Sticky fingers. It was no wonder his friends now limited their invitations to public places only.

"I'm afraid the apartment isn't baby-proofed. You keep your eye on Daisy," she said, "while I put everything out on the table."

"Our food's in the brown bag," he said. "Daisy's is in the red vinyl."

Jeannie peeked inside the zippered bag. "I made her some farina."

"Farina?"

"It's sort of a cross between a mushy noodle and cereal. Babies seem to love it."

"Terrific," he said, smiling up at her. "I'm game if Daisy is."

Five minutes later he and Jeannie were seated at the table. He'd packed a portable baby seat and Daisy proudly sat between them, her chubby hands banging out her own rhythm on the plastic tray in front of her. Jeannie had dug up a red-white-and-blue bib that one of her nephews had used on his last visit and Hunter tied it around Daisy's neck.

"You eat," Jeannie said, pointing toward the array of deli food on the table. "I'd love to feed Daisy."

"Busman's holiday, wouldn't you say? I'd think you'd have your fill of kids at work."

"This is different," Jeannie said. "Daisy's special."

Hunter had made a living selling people things they didn't need. He knew all about flattery, both sincere and otherwise. Still, watching as Jeannie spooned up the farina and fed it to an eager Daisy, he couldn't help but believe she'd meant every word she said.

At least, he hoped she did, although he couldn't say why her opinion should matter. They weren't friends—hell, they barely knew each other.

Although he wouldn't mind remedying that situation. Her T-shirt clung to her breasts just closely enough so he could see they were as round and as firm as he'd imagined. She wasn't wearing a bra and his eyes were drawn repeatedly to the shadowy buds of her nipples pressing against the soft fabric. He wondered how they would feel against his palm as they grew taut and hard with desire, how they would taste as his lips closed around them.

She shifted position slightly as she reached for a cloth to wipe Daisy's mouth and her T-shirt rode up slightly in the back, revealing the curve of her tiny waist. He had no doubt he could span it with his hands and have room to spare.

Get a grip on yourself, Phillips. A Technicolor parade of erotic images were moving across his brain with lightning speed. The way her cheeks would flush with passion...the softness of her skin...the sweet taste of her mouth...the urgent sounds of surrender...the smell of springtime in her hair—

"Hunter?" Jeannie's voice came to him through a mist of sexual heat. "Are you okay?"

"Fine," he muttered, addressing himself to his supper. "Just fine."

He made short work of the pastrami and half a tuna sandwich. There was something to be said for sublimation.

"Better grab a sandwich while you can, Jeannie. The food's disappearing."

She laughed as she wiped the baby's messy face. "Tell me about it. Your daughter has quite an appetite."

"Takes after her mother," Hunter said, relieved to be on more neutral territory. "Callie had an appetite like a lumberjack."

She'd wondered when the subject would come up. "You're a widower?"

He shook his head. "Never married."

"Oh." She busied herself sprinkling pepper on her tuna sandwich and rearranging the pickle slices. It was the 90s, after all. Families didn't necessarily come in the old ideal of mother-father-child any longer. She wondered who the mother was...*where* she was.

"No more questions?"

Her cheeks reddened. "It's none of my business."

"Callie was my sister." He took a deep breath, willing away the stab of pain. "She died giving birth to Daisy."

"Oh, God...Hunter." She was next to him, her hand resting lightly on his shoulder. "I'm so sorry."

"So am I," he said, his voice soft. He'd never forget that phone call in the night...or those terrible words. "She'd been living in Tokyo, working as a translator. I'd been planning to fly there after the baby was born, but—" He felt as if he had a burning rock in the middle of his throat. "When the phone rang that night, I knew. The doctor didn't have to say a damn thing." *I'm sorry, Mr. Phillips. I'm so sorry.*

"What about Daisy's father?"

He shrugged. "According to one of Callie's friends, it might have been an Englishman she'd worked with in Tokyo, but we'll never know for sure." His laugh was bitter. "That biological clock of hers was ticking so loud she couldn't think of anything else. She was determined to have a baby before she turned forty, come hell or high water. The father was immaterial to Callie."

She understood his pain in a way he could never imagine. "The maternal urge is a powerful thing, Hunter. Most women would sacrifice anything for their children."

He met her eyes. "Even their lives?"

"Given the chance."

Something was happening here. Hunter wasn't always the most perceptive of guys, but even he knew something was different. On the surface they were still talking about Callie but he knew that Jeannie's thoughts were somewhere else.

Daisy picked that moment to overturn her bowl of farina.

"That's my girl," he said, grabbing for a napkin to mop up the mess. "Always the center of attention."

Jeannie disappeared into the kitchen, then came back with a roll of paper towels and a wet sponge. "Thank God for Scotchguard. I don't think there's a mother alive who doesn't—" She stopped abruptly, then busied herself cleaning farina off Daisy's foot.

"Look," he said, sitting back on his heels, "you don't have to watch what you say around me. Life goes on. I know that." The truth was, it felt good to talk about Callie. Except for the logistics of caring for Daisy, he'd never talked about his situation, or the emotions involved, with any of his pals at work.

And nobody had ever asked.

"What about your parents?" Jeannie asked, fluffing the nap of the rug with her fingers. "Did they feel they were too old to care for an infant?"

Hunter felt his jaw harden. "They're not too old," he snapped.

"Sorry." Jeannie stood up. "It was none of my business anyway."

"I don't mind talking about it."

"Really?" Her eyebrows lifted. "You could have fooled me."

"It's a long story."

She tossed the used paper towels into the wastebasket near the kitchen door. "I'm not going anywhere."

It was as if he'd been waiting eight months for somebody to say that to him. "My parents have seen Daisy precisely once. They were on their way to the Bahamas and they stopped off to meet their granddaughter." The entire visit had lasted all of fifteen minutes. Daisy, with her blond hair and blue eyes and sunny disposition, was Callie all over again. It had been more than they could bear. "They didn't stop again on their way home."

"Their choice or yours?"

"Theirs. They were visiting Callie in Tokyo when she found out she was pregnant." Daisy dropped her set of plastic keys and Hunter retrieved them. "They took the next plane home." His parents nibbled at the edges of life. Callie had devoured it.

Jeannie felt as if she was making her way across a field of land mines. "Some people have strong feelings about the right way to raise a child."

Briefly, and with a minimum of emotion, he told Jeannie about his parents' almost eerie detachment when he called to tell them of their daughter's death. He'd asked them to accompany him to Tokyo, but they had declined.

"Daisy was twenty-eight-hours old when I got to the hospital." The bittersweet memory tore at his heart. "I hated her on sight."

Jeannie's breath caught and involuntarily she reached out to touch the baby's golden head.

"I would've traded Daisy in a second if it meant getting my sister back." Grief-stricken and jet-lagged, he'd stumbled his way through mountains of red tape. "It took three days," he continued, "but I finally cleared it so I could take Callie back home. I was halfway to the airport when I remembered." *Daisy.* Callie's death had obliterated everything else from his mind. "Daisy was still in the hospital nursery." The temptation to run had been strong. "I didn't want a kid. I liked my life exactly the way it was. Things at C V & S were beginning to move and I knew I'd managed to find my way onto the fast track. But it was me or it was nobody."

Jeannie didn't know Hunter well, but she understood what was happening. The anger. The pain. The overwhelming need to recount every detail. She'd been there herself not that long ago.

She sat down on her chair and rested her elbows on the table. Daisy was busy playing with her colorful set of plastic keys. Hunter seemed lost in memories.

"Daisy peed on me for the first time somewhere between Japan and Hawaii. That's when I knew we were stuck with each other." His parents were locked in their own world of grief. He had no brothers or sisters. "I'd toyed with the idea of finding some nice young couple to adopt her. I even called a few lawyers I knew to see how I could locate a great family for Daisy, but when push came to shove, I couldn't do it." This was his sister's daughter. Callie lived on in that helpless infant and, in a way, so did he. Only a coldhearted bastard would turn away from her, even if there were days when he was certain he was exactly that.

"I'm not father material," he stated bluntly. "I never figured I'd hook on with anybody for the long haul, much less raise a baby."

"You did the right thing," Jeannie said, her voice soft. "You acted from the heart."

The look he gave her was sharply skeptical. "We went through five housekeepers in the first six weeks," he went on. "They talked about schedules and charts—" He shook his head at the memory. "The last one said to just let her cry."

"I hope you fired her immediately," Jeannie said, outraged on Daisy's behalf.

"Her butt was out the door before she finished the sentence. I don't know much about kids, but I know cruelty when I hear it."

"Do you have a housekeeper now?"

He shook his head. "The last one went back to Ireland to be with her daughter. What I need is a rent-a-wife."

"How do you manage? I've worked for enough ad agencies to know they're not exactly sympathetic to family problems." How many times had she seen babies and little children treated with a disregard that made her blood run cold?

"I don't manage," said Hunter. "At least, not lately. Daisy's been sharing my office for the past two weeks."

"The powers-that-be must love that."

"It's getting pretty dicey," Hunter admitted. "Portable car seats and cribs don't exactly fit the agency's image. Now that they're applying pressure, I don't know how much longer I can drag this out." Not to mention the ambition that had been put on hold and ate at his gut every day as he saw his future slipping away from him.

"What do you mean, applying pressure?" This was smoother emotional terrain. She motioned for him to follow her into the kitchen where she began to prepare the coffee.

Hunter leaned against the doorjamb between kitchen and dining room, so he could keep his eye on Daisy and continue his conversation with Jeannie. "Grantham is sending me on a four-night cruise Thursday to oversee a shoot for the cruise line."

"Tough duty," said Jeannie as she measured coffee into the filter. "My heart goes out to you."

He shot her a look. "Try that with an eight-month-old there with you."

She pushed the button on the automatic coffee maker then perched on the countertop, feet dangling, to wait. "Isn't there someone who could watch Daisy while you're away?"

"No one I'd trust for that long."

"Friends? Family?"

"My family's in California and my friends think babies exist only in commercials. I'm between a rock and a hard place—exactly where Grantham wants me."

You could do it, whispered a small voice that Jeannie was doing her best to ignore. *You could watch her for the weekend.* She cleared her throat. "I wish I could help you, but..." She let her words trail off delicately. Dangerous territory, this. It had been so long since she had someone to care for. It was the last thing she needed.

"I wouldn't ask you." His words were blunt, decisive. For some reason they felt like a slap. "Daisy's my responsibility. I'm not going to foist her off on a stranger so I can go off on a cruise."

An uneasy silence settled between them. The rush of water through the coffee machine sounded like Niagara Falls. Jeannie shifted uncomfortably, aware that she'd sat in a puddle of water her dish towel had missed. She must have sounded like a prime candidate for a rubber room before, telling him that she couldn't possibly take care of Daisy. They barely knew each other. Why on earth would he even consider asking her to watch his little girl?

In the other room, Daisy gurgled happily as she played with her plastic keys.

"I've never seen such a good-natured baby before," said Jeannie in an attempt to fill the uncomfortable silence. "Is she always this even tempered?"

"Pretty much. I've been told teething will put an end to it."

Conversation skidded to a halt once again. The phone rang and Jeannie leaped to answer it, certain that Hunter was as grateful for the interruption as she was.

Hunter scooped Daisy up from her chair and walked with her into the living room to give Jeannie some privacy. It wasn't like him to talk like that with a stranger. Not even his closest pals at work knew the full story about Callie and his parents.

You didn't talk about your emotions where he came from. People like his parents kept their emotions bottled up inside where they belonged. There was something unpleasant about emotional displays, something almost un-American. He'd always envied people with unpronounceable last names who sang at the top of their lungs and danced on tabletops and drained every last drop from the bottle then asked for more.

Like his sister.

He walked over to the window that overlooked the tree-lined street. Daisy yawned and nestled her head against his shoulder. He knew the exact second when she dropped off to sleep by the way her breathing slowed and her little hands relaxed their grip on his shirt. Her tiny thumbs played out a rhythm against his chest and he remembered the way Callie's foot had tapped out a secret code as she watched television when they were kids.

He wondered if Daisy would be like his sister, one

of the lucky ones who knew how to live life to the fullest.

Callie had been all fire and brilliance, blazing through his parents' life like a comet. She'd lived at a fever pitch, as if she'd known her time was limited and she had to experience everything she possibly could before it was too late. They'd tried everything they could to tame her fire, but that had been like trying to lasso the sun.

Jeannie's laughter floated out from the kitchen. It occurred to him that the scene was like something from a 1950s sitcom—if you didn't know better. Mom making coffee. Dad relaxing after dinner. Baby sound asleep.

Not that family life appealed to him particularly. Before Daisy, he'd been content to pretty much go where the wind blew. Work had been the focus of his life and he'd been happy to offer up everything on the altar of ambition.

He'd never yearned for home and hearth—maybe because as a kid he'd found the reality to be strangely empty.

The rich smell of fresh coffee drifted toward him. Jeannie had finished her telephone conversation and he heard the clink of cups and saucers as she bustled around the kitchen. When she told him where she lived, he'd been expecting one of those minimalist artsy places like his, with charcoal-gray walls and thick white leather sofas, but Jeannie had surprised him. This was the kind of place where a man could get comfortable. He glanced around at the living room. Overstuffed sofas and chairs. Lots of flowery fabric. A big wood-burning fireplace with real wood in it, not that prefab garbage that sent off pink and green yuppie flames.

In fact, everything about Jeannie Ross seemed as genuine as that wood-burning fireplace. The fact that she was also sexy as hell was a bonus.

During their meal he'd spent an inordinate amount of time cataloguing her physical attributes. The shape of her breasts, the curve of her waist, the silkiness of her hair. But her sexuality went beyond the obvious. She lived easily within her own skin, as if the trappings of beauty touched her only lightly if at all. She was a toucher, a giver, the kind of woman who made you forget the world was a cold and lonely place.

Too bad she wasn't his type.

"Sorry I took so long." She glided into the living room, carrying a tray. "I was supposed to meet my friend Kate for dinner and I completely forgot."

He glanced at his watch. "It's not even eight o'clock yet. Why don't Daisy and I shove off and maybe you can—"

"Don't be silly." She placed the tray on the square coffee table and sat down on the couch. "I'm on vacation now, remember? Six whole weeks with absolutely nothing to do but relax. We're going to have breakfast tomorrow instead."

He made a nest of pillows for Daisy then sat down opposite Jeannie. Her movements were casually elegant as she poured coffee into two thick red cups.

"I can offer you cream, sugar, and whatever artificial ingredient your heart desires."

"Black."

"A purist." She handed him a cup, then added a spoonful of sugar to her own. "I have no willpower when it comes to sugar."

"Pizza's my downfall," said Hunter. "Extra cheese, onions, and pepperoni. As soon as Daisy has teeth, I'm going to introduce her first slice."

She sipped her coffee. "You like being a father, don't you?"

"I love Daisy," he said, helping himself to a handful of chocolate chip cookies, "but I'm not her father."

"You are in the ways that matter."

"Maybe, but that doesn't change the fact that she's my niece, not my daughter."

"To her, you're daddy."

"Scary stuff," he said after a moment. "These days I'm lucky to be able to find socks that match." The responsibility of raising a child was overwhelming. "Who knows? One day her real father might show up on the doorstep and stake his claim." It would be up to Hunter to step aside—something that would be the best for everyone concerned.

"I don't think that's about to happen."

"Who knows," said Hunter. "I've given up guessing what the future has in store for me."

"You know, despite everything you're really a lucky man. Out of something terrible, came something pretty wonderful. It doesn't always happen that way.''

There was a change in the tone of her voice, a certain wistfulness that caught his attention. He wondered if she'd ever known heartache. She looked to be somewhere around his age. The odds were she hadn't sailed through life without experiencing a storm or two, but the storms hadn't marked her in any way that he could discern.

Daisy awakened and Hunter changed her while Jeannie warmed up a bottle. She insisted that she be allowed to feed Daisy and Hunter watched as she expertly gave the baby her bottle.

"You're good," he observed. "Is it part of the job description?"

"Sometimes," she said, adjusting the dish towel draped over her shoulder. "Depending on the account involved, I could be anything from mother substitute to traffic cop to court jester."

Daisy burped loudly and they both laughed.

"So what are you going to do with your six weeks off?" Hunter asked as Daisy's blue eyes began to close.

"Nothing much," said Jeannie with a sigh. "I'd been thinking of going to Bermuda, but I still haven't managed to get a passport. I suppose I'll just putter around the apartment and catch up on my reading."

And that was when the idea hit him.

"Why don't you come with me?"

"To Bermuda?"

"To nowhere."

"What?"

"A cruise to nowhere. The more I think about it, the more sense it makes. I don't know why I didn't come up with this sooner. My problems are over."

"You've lost me, Hunter. Back up a few paces and start again."

"I have to work. You're on vacation. Daisy needs someone to watch her. It's simple."

"Not to me it isn't."

"It's like this." He leaned forward, elbows on his knees, and fixed her with a look. "I can't leave Daisy home. You'd like to get away for a few days. The agency booked a two bedroom cabin for me on the cruise ship we're representing." He leaned back, the picture of male contentment. "It's perfect."

"Perfect for you," said Jeannie, rising to her feet. "I don't know what your deal is, Hunter, but at least now I know why you wanted to have dinner with me." The look she gave him was filled with reproach. "Thanks but no thanks. Find yourself another baby-sitter. This one's on vacation."

"Maybe I'm not saying this right." Hunter cast about for a new angle. "The commercial for the *Star of the Atlantic* has to be perfect or I'm history."

"We all have our problems. These days nobody's job is secure."

"Right," he said, heartened that he'd at least got this far. "That's not the end of the world when you have only yourself to think about. Look, I don't expect you to understand, but when you have a kid to consider, it's Armageddon."

Jeannie felt her defenses weaken. The last thing she needed was to let herself become emotionally involved with Daisy—or with her father. But there was something so appealingly sincere about his expression that she almost forgot he was an advertising exec. "Of course I understand, but I'm afraid I don't see what's in it for me."

"A cruise," he said, gaining enthusiasm. "A chance to kick back and relax. Meet new people."

"Advertising types? No thanks." She could just imagine the gossip mill working overtime, linking her and Hunter together in some romantic liaison.

"I'm the only advertising type going," he said. "All expenses paid, Jeannie. Think of it as a vacation."

"Right. A vacation with an eight-month-old."

"I'll be there, too," he reminded her. "When I'm not working, she's my responsibility. You can do whatever you want." Jeannie was a great-looking woman. He wasn't about to commandeer all of her free time—especially since she'd made it obvious he wasn't her type at all. "There are no strings involved, if that's what you're worrying about. I'm too tired these days to put the moves on Michelle Pfeiffer."

"Thanks for the compliment," she drawled, a half smile on her face. She remembered the busty blond model he'd been eyeing at the agency that morning. Small brunettes were obviously not his style. He'd already told her he was ambitious. For all she knew this could be a ploy designed to win her over to his side.

It was working.

"I'll think about it."

"I can't ask for more than that, can I?"

"You probably can," she said, "but I wouldn't advise it."

"You think I'm being pushy, don't you?"

"Obnoxious is more like it. Charming at times, but obnoxious."

"Comes with the territory," he said with a shrug of his broad shoulders. "Survival of the fittest at C V & S. Believe it or not, I can be a pretty decent guy under more normal circumstances."

"I'll have to take your word for that."

Hunter polished off a second cup of coffee then stood up. "I was out of line," he said, beginning to gather up Daisy's belongings. "Forget I said anything. I'm grasping at straws these days anyway." He pitched the empty bottle and blanket into his carryall. "I still owe you dinner for taking care of Daisy during the shoot this morning."

"Taking care of adorable babies is what I do for a living," she said. "No special thanks necessary."

Hunter knew an impasse when he saw one. The lady wasn't interested. Time to say good-night and goodbye. She plucked Daisy from the nest of pillows and held her close. He noticed the way she cradled the baby's head—and the kiss she'd pressed to Daisy's cheek when she thought he wasn't looking.

"Take care, Jeannie Ross," he said as he claimed his daughter at the door.

"You, too, Hunter Phillips."

And that, he supposed, was that.

AND IT MIGHT HAVE BEEN, if it weren't for the keys.

Jeannie was getting ready for bed a few hours later when she saw them peeking out from under the skirt of the sofa. Daisy's colorful plastic keys.

Smiling, she crouched down and retrieved them.

"Oh, Daisy," she said out loud, jingling the keys together. "What are you going to do without your toy?"

She glanced at the clock. A little after eleven. Hunter might be asleep by now. Daisy most certainly was. First thing in the morning she'd ring him at the office and let him know Daisy's keys were safe and sound.

If only she had a quarter for every favorite toy she'd rescued these past few years for one of her show-business charges. Stuffed dogs with floppy ears. Big cuddly pandas. Security blankets, silver rattles, and dolls of all descriptions.

Christy and Sara had been no exceptions. If Jeannie closed her eyes, she could summon up the image of the big old terry-cloth dinosaur that they had loved to distraction. "No, Mommy, no!" they'd cried each time she had to pry Dino away from them in order to wash it.

"He won't be gone forever," she would say with a laugh. "Didn't Daddy tell you—"

She blinked her eyes, willing herself back into the present. Daisy and Hunter's plight had reached her more deeply than she'd imagined, stirring up memories from her long-ago life. There was no way he

could have known how his story would affect her—
no one could have. She'd been hard on him before
when he'd suggested she join them on the cruise to
nowhere, but not for the reason she'd given. The truth
was, she'd wanted nothing more than to throw caution
to the winds and say yes.

The oddest thing had happened to her this morning
when she first saw him. She'd been sitting up on the
ladder waiting for Amanda Bennett and her mom to
show up when Hunter burst from the set, Daisy in his
arms, and the feeling settled itself around her heart.
His dark hair brushed the back of his collar. His tie
was askew. A wet spot was spreading across his
pants, thanks, no doubt, to the picture-perfect baby in
his arms.

Her breath had caught in her throat. She saw beautiful babies every day at work—and beautiful men as
well. But there was something about those two that
reached deep inside her heart and touched the part of
her soul that few people knew existed, making her
feel as if she were awakening from a long sleep.

Not that it mattered, she thought. Smart women
didn't go away with total strangers. Hunter was brash,
opinionated, opportunistic in the way of all good advertising men. Not at all her type. Yet there was
something else, a basic decency that made everything
else seem unimportant. He might not consider himself
to be Daisy's father, but one look at the way he cared
for that little girl had told her otherwise.

She felt as if she was awakening from a deep sleep,
stretching her arms toward the sun as her eyes grew

accustomed to the light. Logic told her that going away with Hunter was absolutely crazy. He and Daisy had managed without her for eight months. They could manage four days at sea.

Her heart, however, demanded to be heard.

Do it, Jeannie. Throw caution to the winds and take a chance.

She was tired of being alone, tired of listening to the sound of her heart beating at night in the still apartment, tired of wondering why the fates had seen fit to spare her and not the ones she loved.

It wasn't every day an opportunity like this dropped into your lap, she reasoned. Maybe it was time to stop watching other people having all the fun and have some fun herself.

Chapter Three

The next morning Hunter called Baby Minders, Nannies-To-Go, and the sister of one of his basketball pals, but to no avail. It would have been easier to find Amelia Earhart than to find someone to take care of Daisy on the cruise ship this coming weekend. As soon as they heard he was a single man, they bailed out.

Daisy had a noontime appointment at the pediatrician for a checkup, so it was a little after two o'clock when Hunter returned to the office.

Lisa, his assistant, looked up from her computer. "Haines called twice," she said, pushing her trendy glasses to the top of her head. "He wants the figures on the Amstar deal."

Hunter groaned as he bent down for Lisa to take Daisy from the backpack he wore. "Who doesn't? Call accounting and see what you can shake out of them." He started for his office.

"Jeannie Ross called." Eyes twinkling, she handed Daisy over to him. "Anything I should know about?"

"Get back to work, Lisa." He stalked into his office and closed the door behind him. It took a few minutes to get Daisy settled down in her portable car seat, then a few minutes longer to get through to Jeannie.

"I have Daisy's key ring," she said after the usual pleasantries.

He leaned back in his chair and propped his feet up on the desk. "Terrific. I turned the house inside-out last night."

"If you'd like, I'll drop it off with your doorman."

"I'll pick it up after work," he said, genuinely pleased to hear her voice. "Why should you go to the trouble?"

A short silence, then: "Fine."

So much for scintillating conversation. He'd never met a woman as immune to his attempts at charm as Jeannie Ross. It was enough to depress the hell out of a man.

He cleared his throat. "Don't worry if you have to go out. You can leave the keys with *your* doorman."

"He's on vacation. If you tell me what time you'll be here, I'll make sure I'm around."

"You know C V & S," he said with a short laugh. "The hours are nine to infinity. Don't sit there waiting on my account."

In her apartment, Jeannie stared at the telephone in dismay. This wasn't going the way she'd planned. He sounded as if he couldn't wait to get off the phone. Was it possible that he'd found someone else to watch Daisy?

"Listen," she began carefully, "I've been thinking about what you said last night."

In his office Hunter sat up straight in his chair. "About the cruise?"

"Yes," said Jeannie. Another beat pause. "Do you still need someone to watch Daisy?"

"More than ever." He told her about the visit to the pediatrician and the tooth that was ready to erupt any moment.

"Call me crazy," said Jeannie, "but you can count me in."

"You'll go?"

Her laugh curled itself inside his ear. Soft, sexy, womanly. *Forget it, Phillips. This is the baby-sitter you're talking about here. The one who's not interested.*

"I can't believe I'm saying this but yes, I'll go."

"We have to talk about money. I'm not asking you to do this for nothing."

"We'll get around to it," she said, her voice light. "Right now I'm more concerned with when and where."

He riffled through some papers on his desk and found the itinerary.

"Thursday morning at the pier," she said, repeating the number. "See you then."

"Well, Daisy," said Hunter as he hung up the phone. "It looks like life's about to get very interesting."

JEANNIE SPENT the next few days in a blur of activity. There was laundry to do, dry cleaning to pick up, errands to run. She was so busy that she barely had time to give the reason for all that activity a second thought.

Which was probably a good thing because if she did give it a second thought, she might have backed out on the deal.

The night before she even dragged her pal Kate Mullen to a boutique near Bloomingdale's to help her settle on one drop-dead cocktail dress. She couldn't remember the last time she bought a dress simply because it was beautiful and the experience was downright intoxicating.

"Look at this one," she said, pirouetting before the dressing room mirror. "Spaghetti straps, tight waist, dance skirt."

"That dress means business," said Kate. "I thought you weren't interested in him."

"A woman can't buy a dress just because it's gorgeous?"

"Not a dress like that. That one has seduction written all over it."

A ripple of excitement raced up Jeannie's spine. "I'm not his type, Kate. He likes them young, blond, and brainless."

"You're not just saying that so I won't worry about you, are you?"

She pirouetted once again before the mirror. "He was crazy about that ditsy model they'd hired for the Fancy Pants commercial." *But he asked you to din-*

ner, a little voice whispered. *And you're the one who's going on the cruise with him.*

"You're crazy," said Kate. "Only a crazy person would do something like this."

"So I'm crazy," said Jeannie, enjoying the notion. "Everyone's entitled to one moment of insanity."

"The guy's in advertising," said Kate. "He tells lies for a living."

Jeannie turned to face her friend. "Don't you think you're making too much of it, Kate? Four measly nights on a cruise ship and you're acting like I'm running away to join the circus."

"The circus would make more sense. At least there's a future in it."

"I'm not looking for a future. The guy needs help. I have the time and the expertise." She whirled back to the mirror to admire her dress. "And I get a boat ride in the bargain. I can't lose."

Kate, an unemployed stand-up comedienne, launched into a hilariously wicked diatribe against single men on the prowl that had Jeannie laughing out loud despite herself.

"Good thing I'm not looking for a man," she said, reaching for the zipper of her dress.

Kate frowned. "Then why are you buying that dress?"

"Because it's black lace, it's expensive, and I love it."

"Hope springs eternal," said Kate with a sigh. "Even for those of us over thirty and never married."

Jeannie cast her friend a sharp look, then glanced away. *If you only knew the whole story, Kate....*

"I'LL REMEMBER YOU for this, Grantham," Hunter muttered as he struggled to cram six more diapers into the duffel bag. He'd always known his boss was a devious SOB, but this proved it.

"Daahh?"

He glanced over at Daisy who was strapped into her car seat and perched on the floor near the luggage.

"Don't even think about it," he warned with mock solemnity. "That's a new diaper you're wearing."

Daisy stared at him wide-eyed. He always wondered how much she actually understood. "More than you think," the pediatrician had said when Hunter asked. "She's a little sponge, soaking up everything you can give her."

At first Hunter had felt like a jerk, talking out loud to an infant whose main concerns in life were food and sleep. But the more he talked to her, the easier it got and now he found himself carrying on a running monologue with the little girl that he figured would come back to haunt him in ten or fifteen years.

"Okay," he said, "clothes, diapers, bottles, food." Not to mention car seat, toys, and bouncing baby girl.

All he had to do was get everything downstairs, into the cab, and aboard ship in that order.

And then work a miracle or two.

"MR. PHILLIPS, I'm afraid we simply can't wait a second longer."

"Five more minutes," Hunter said, peering down

at the dock below. "She'll be here."

The purser, a lean man in his fifties, looked at Hunter with a combination of pity and disdain. "I'll speak to the harbormaster about delaying, but I can't guarantee anything, given the tides and all." The purser hurried off.

"She wouldn't back out on us without calling, would she, Daisy?" he asked the baby who was strapped into the ubiquitous backpack. Everything he'd heard about Jeannie Ross said that she was as responsible as she was lovely, a rarity in advertising circles. When Jeannie Ross took a job, you knew she'd not only be on time, she'd be ten minutes early.

An ambulance siren sounded in the distance. What if something had happened to her? New York was a rough city and she hadn't been in town very long. What if she'd decided to do something crazy like take the long way through Central Park?

He spun around, ready to find the recalcitrant purser and ask him to call the police and the hospitals, only to find himself face-to-face with Jeannie. She was weighed down with suitcases. A huge leather tote was slung over her shoulder, making her list to starboard.

"Where the hell have you been?" he bellowed over waves of intense relief. "The whole damn ship is looking for you."

She dropped her bags to the deck with a resounding crash. "No wonder," she snapped right back. The woman might be small but she was feisty. "You might've tried giving me the right pier number."

He wasn't about to be stopped by logic. "They're holding up the departure for you. I'd better tell the purser you finally showed up."

"Don't bother. I ran into him near the gangway. Everything's cool."

This isn't going to be easy, thought Hunter. *She's illogical and she has a temper besides.*

Typical male, thought Jeannie. *He'd rather eat nails than admit he made a mistake.*

They jumped as two blasts of the ship's horn split the air.

"Glad you've found each other," said the purser as he approached, clipboard in hand. "We're on our way."

Jeannie and Hunter looked at each other with growing alarm.

Short of jumping overboard, they were now stuck with each other for the next five days. They watched in silence as the tug eased the ship toward open waters.

"I thought they threw streamers," said Jeannie.

"Only in movies," Hunter said.

"This should be festive and exciting," she continued, undaunted by his lack of interest. "Going on a cruise is a big deal for most people. Where are the bon voyage parties and the glamour?"

"Like the *Love Boat,* I suppose?"

"Absolutely. Cruises are about fantasy." She glanced at him with curiosity. "I'm surprised you didn't think of that, Hunter, being in advertising and all.''

He grunted something noncommittal. He wasn't in the mood to admit it to her, but she had a point. A little pomp and circumstance wouldn't hurt. He'd have to remember to add that to his report after they got settled in their suite.

"Why don't we check out the cabin?" he asked as a light rain began to fall.

"Good idea," said Jeannie. "I'd like to get unpacked and let Daisy adjust to her new bed before naptime."

Finding their way through the labyrinthine corridors required a compass and a guide.

"We're on the wrong deck," said Jeannie, checking her yellow ticket. "This is B. We want C."

"This is C," said Hunter. "The walls are painted green."

"The green walls are on B Deck. C has yellow walls." She waved her ticket at him. "See? They're color coordinated."

Hunter muttered something dark.

"I wish you'd stop that," Jeannie said as they made their way up the carpeted staircase to C deck.

"Stop what?"

"Muttering under your breath. It's rude."

He held the door for her. "Don't push it, Ross. We still have four days to go."

She stopped in the doorway. "And what's that supposed to mean?"

"Don't ask."

"I *am* asking. It's not my fault I got here late. It's yours."

He said nothing. The truth was, the sight of her in her short red skirt and white tank top had him sweating bullets. Who would've thought a tiny woman would have such long legs?

And who would have imagined she'd fill out that skimpy top in such an alarming fashion.

Over the past few days he'd done his best to convince himself that Jeannie Ross was just your everyday average woman. He'd had himself believing it, too. He'd told himself her hair was just an average dark brown, not shimmering black satin, that her eyes were run-of-the-mill blue, and not the color of faceted sapphires. Droplets of rain glistened on her cheeks and trembled on her lashes. He wondered what she would do if he licked them off.

She was walking ahead of him down the corridor, her fanny swaying from side to side, making promises she didn't even know about.

Make it a big suite, he prayed. *Steel doors between their bedrooms.* Separate bathrooms so he wouldn't have to see her panty hose drying on the shower rod.

Of course, maybe she didn't wear panty hose. Maybe she wore one of those frilly garter belts with roses embroidered on them and sleek black silk stockings made to be seen by a man who—

"Daah?" Daisy tugged hard at his ear. It was almost as effective as a cold shower.

"Here it is." Jeannie stopped in front of a door. "Do you have the key?"

He reached into his shirt pocket, then withdrew one of those credit-card style keys. He inserted it into the slot, waited a moment for the green light to appear, then swung open the door.

"Ohmigod!" Jeannie sounded the way he felt.

"We've got a problem," said Hunter.

Jeannie glanced around. "I'll say we do."

"I told them the other day that we weren't—I mean, that we're not—" *Sleeping together*. Why didn't he just say it?

"I know what you mean," said Jeannie, plucking Daisy from his backpack. "Too bad they didn't." The tiny suite definitely had been designed for a couple who knew each other in the biblical sense—or was about to. Rough seas could put them in a compromising position.

He sank onto one of the tiny chairs flanking the even tinier couch. "Who'd they think were planning to stay here—a pair of Munchkins?"

She ran a hand across a minuscule desk bolted to the wall beneath the porthole. "At least Daisy will be right at home." She met Hunter's eyes. "What are we going to do? We can't possibly stay here together." The suite did have two bedrooms, but they might as well knock down the thin wall between them for all the privacy it offered. She and Hunter would be in each other's hair every moment of the day.

"I'll go talk to the purser. There has to be something else available."

There wasn't.

"We've given you the finest accommodations we

have,'' the purser said, not looking up from his computer terminal.

"I realize that," Hunter said, struggling with his temper. "Maybe you could give us two cheap rooms, next to each other."

"We're booked up," the purser said sternly. "The Cruise-to-Nowhere is our most popular event."

Hunter offered the man a crisp hundred-dollar bill but the purser remained adamant. He considered offering a condo in Hawaii in exchange for another cabin, but he had the distinct feeling the purser was enjoying his troubles.

Hunter made his way back to the cabin feeling as though he was on the last leg of the Bataan Death March.

Great, he thought as he approached the suite where Jeannie and Daisy were waiting for him. Here he was, telling her the trip was strictly business, when everything about the tiny cabin screamed otherwise—and now he had to tell her they were stuck there. Talk about being between a rock and a hard place....

"No dice," he said as he stepped inside the drawing room. "I wouldn't blame you if you jumped overboard."

She stared at him in horror. "Do you mean we're stuck in this floating telephone booth?"

"Afraid so."

She slumped back on the chair while Daisy crawled happily around the room.

"I screwed up," he said, still standing in the doorway. "I'll use the suite during the day and sleep in the lounge at night."

Jeannie had been ready to read him the riot act. Living in such close proximity with a stranger and an eight-month-old baby was a surefire prescription for disaster. She'd expected him to storm back to the room, all male bluster and outrage, casting blame everywhere but where it belonged: on himself.

Did he have to be so accommodating? So understanding?

So gorgeous...

"You can't sleep in the lounge, Hunter." Even though any sane person would certainly think about it. "This suite is yours, not mine."

"You're not going to sleep in the lounge, Jeannie."

"I wasn't suggesting that." She leaned forward. "We're both adults. We should be able to coexist for a few days, wouldn't you say?"

He looked like a man who'd received a stay of execution. "I should've known," he said, shaking his head. "I can't believe I fell for advertising hype."

Jeannie laughed as she reached down to guide Daisy away from a basket of flowers resting on the floor. "Poetic justice, I'd say." They both knew advertising was all about illusion. Promise 'em everything but deliver the bare minimum.

"Their ad copy calls this a 'spacious suite.'"

"'Spacious' is in the eye of the beholder."

"I'd like to get my hands around the beholder's neck." There was barely room to take a deep breath in the hallway.

"We need a system," said Jeannie. "Why don't you check your schedule and we can figure out a way to save our privacy." *And our sanity.*

He rummaged through his briefcase, then withdrew a battered leather organizer. "Son of a—we'll have to talk later," he said, heading for the door. "Got a meeting with the activities director."

"Great schedule, Phillips," Jeannie muttered as the door closed behind him.

"Daaah?" said Daisy.

Jeannie looked down at the golden-haired baby. "You're right, Daisy. He fights dirty."

BY THE TIME Jeannie unpacked both her things and Daisy's, Hunter had returned to the suite to work. Sitting on the edge of the bed in the room she shared with Daisy, she listened as he grumbled and tossed papers around. She had to use the bathroom, which was on the opposite side of the suite, but decided she'd rather die than use it while he was around. The fact that that could prove problematic before the trip was over wasn't lost on her.

"You're lucky," she said to Daisy who was sitting in the middle of the bed, playing with her ring of plastic keys. "Diapers can solve a multitude of problems."

She got up and walked to the door. Hunter was hunched over a growing stack of papers, looking harried and unhappy. If the situation wasn't so downright weird, she'd actually feel sorry for him. "I'm going to change Daisy and go exploring.'' *And maybe find a bathroom.*

"Great," Hunter mumbled, absorbed in the paper he was reading.

"We might check out the indoor wading pool."

"Mmmph," said Hunter.

"I might strip naked, jump in, and do the back stroke."

"Have fun."

See, Kate? she thought as she went back into the bedroom. *I could be Winston Churchill for all he cares.*

Which made things a lot easier. She should thank her lucky stars he was going to keep his part of their bargain.

She dressed Daisy in a pink T-shirt, head band, and hot-pink ruffled pants pulled on over her diaper. She slipped out of her skirt and tank top and donned a simple bright red swimsuit and coverup.

"We're leaving," she said as she and Daisy headed for the door. "I don't know when we'll be back."

He barely looked up. "Have fun."

"We'll do our best."

Hunter waited until the door closed behind her and he heard her footsteps fading away. A vision of how she'd looked in that snug swimsuit sizzled before his eyes. That short robe of hers hadn't quite covered the rounded curves of her derriere.

She looked too damn good. She should be thirty years older and thirty pounds heavier. Maybe then living together in this cracker box cabin wouldn't be the exercise in torture that he suspected it was going to be.

"Get a grip, man," he said out loud. Centuries of evolution had made it possible for a male to sublimate his desire for a female—at least long enough to build a civilization or two. He could hang on to his hormones long enough to put together an ad campaign.

By that time they'd be back in New York. He'd go his way. She'd go hers.

And life would be back to normal.

Chapter Four

It worked for an hour.

Hunter was able to put Jeannie out of his mind while he roughed out a sketch for a print ad based on his conversation with the activities director. He also made a few notes on bon voyage celebrations, per Jeannie's comments earlier that morning.

He told himself it wasn't Jeannie he was thinking about, it was Daisy. He could count on one hand the times he'd been separated from her. It wouldn't hurt to wander down to the indoor pool and check up on them both. If he happened to catch Jeannie wandering around in that second-skin bathing suit of hers—well, you can't be convicted for your thoughts, could you?

Besides, he'd been working hard all morning. He deserved a break. He didn't have another meeting until after lunch.

The indoor pool was situated two floors below deck in an enormous, glassed-in area featuring real palm trees, island music, and manufactured sunshine. A lone lap swimmer was Australian-crawling his way from one end of the pool to the other. Two teenage girls in skimpy bathing suits sat at one end, feet dangling in the water. They cast a limpid glance in his direction, then giggled uproariously.

The wading pool was at the far end of the room. Daisy's babyish giggles floated across the humid air, mingling with Jeannie's throaty woman's laugh. Jeannie was seated in the pool with Daisy held firmly on her lap. *Lucky Daisy,* he thought with a grin. All in all, he wouldn't mind trading places with her.

He couldn't make out the words Jeannie was saying to Daisy, but he understood the gentle sound of her voice as she encouraged Daisy in her play. His little girl splashed gleefully, bringing her chubby hands down flat against the surface of the water, then laughing as the spray soaked her and Jeannie both.

"Looks like she's having fun," he said, noting the outline of her nipples, taut and hard, against the wet bathing suit.

"She's not the only one." She brushed her dark hair off her forehead. "Care to join us?"

He motioned toward his slacks and shirt. "I'm not dressed for wading pools."

"Sure you are. Kick off your shoes and roll up your pant legs."

First the Armani jacket, now his best pants. Another year of parenthood and he'd be reduced to wearing rags and begging on street corners.

"What the hell," he said, doing as Jeannie suggested.

Daisy squealed in delight as he sat down on the

edge. She brought her hand down hard and the next second Hunter was soaked from head to toe.

"I can't believe she did that to me," he said, in amazement. "She's only eight months old."

"Your little girl's growing up, Hunter. Before you know it she'll be walking and talking and asking for the keys to the car."

He shuddered and Jeannie laughed.

"I'll settle for getting her toilet trained. I'm not in a rush for the rest of it."

"It happens in the blink of an eye," she said as he sat Daisy on his knee. "But you'll be so busy you won't even realize it's happening."

"You sound like the voice of experience. On-the-job training?"

She wrapped her arms around her knees. He couldn't help but notice her skin was that same shade of pale peach all over. "That and eight nieces and nephews."

"Eight?" He whistled low. "How many brothers and sisters do you have?"

"Five," she said. "Three brothers, one sister."

"Still up in Minnesota?"

"Every single one of them, except me. I've been just about everywhere the past few years with the job."

She told him about her brothers who owned a factory up in Lake of the Woods, and her parents, who were retired but ran a bed and breakfast each summer just for fun. "And then there's Angie," she said, smiling at the thought of her older sister. "Wife, mother, and mayor of Landview township."

"Do you get back there often?"

Her smile faltered but before that fact could register on him, she was her bright and breezy self again. "With my schedule, I'm lucky I get back to the apartment every night."

It occurred to Hunter that with six weeks off she could travel around the world, much less find her way back to northern Minnesota.

None of your business, Phillips. For all he knew, her family was as fractured as his.

"You know what I'd love?" she asked, a big smile on her face. He couldn't remember the last time he'd seen a woman this lovely without makeup.

"Your own cabin," he said wryly.

"Besides that." She scrambled to her feet. He followed the line of her body from ankle to shapely calf to firm thigh then stopped. The simple one-piece red swimsuit managed to reveal more than it concealed, a fact for which he would be forever grateful.

"Five minutes in that gorgeous pool."

"Go ahead," he said. He was disappointed, but he did his best to hide it. The odds of her saying, "Take me, master," had been pretty slim. He'd promised she'd have free time whenever he was available to care for Daisy. He couldn't reneg on the deal just because he was enjoying her company.

Jeannie was a pleasure to watch. She pierced the water cleanly, propelling herself with swift sure strokes that left barely a ripple in her wake. He liked the way she swam, all grace and assurance and lithe strength. Some men said you could tell how a woman would be in bed if you watched how they moved and, from where he sat, Jeannie's moves were pretty damn good.

He stood up, Daisy tucked in the crook of his arm. Not even twenty-four hours into their arrangement and he was entertaining X-rated fantasies about Daisy's baby-sitter. Dangerous territory. He thought he'd put that whole issue aside, but there it was, staring him right in the face. He'd have to keep his libido in check, even if it meant lots of cold showers over the next few days.

He made his way to the side of the pool and waited until Jeannie reached the edge where he was standing.

"I'll go back to the cabin and get Daisy cleaned up."

She began to scramble from the pool.

"Stay," he said. *Please.* "I have a four o'clock meeting. Just be back by then."

She shook the water from her eyes with a quick toss of her head. "There's no reason we can't make this work, Hunter." She fixed him with one of those direct looks with which he was becoming accustomed. "We should be able to stay out of each other's way for a few days." Her arms glistened with droplets of water as she rested her elbows on the ledge.

"I agree," said Hunter, amazed a bolt of lightning didn't strike him dead right there on the spot. "We're both adults, right?"

Jeannie nodded. "Right."

JEANNIE WATCHED as Hunter and Daisy headed back to the cabin the three of them shared.

"I lied," she said as the door swung shut behind them. "It's not going to be easy at all."

And the fact that they were adults was the problem.

He was tall, dark, and handsome; successful, single, and father of a beautiful little girl who was quickly wrapping Jeannie around her tiny finger.

The fact that he could be obnoxious and overbearing was beginning to matter less and less.

But you're not his type, she thought, pushing off from the wall and into the speed lane. *He likes them big and blond.*

"Who cares?" she said, climbing from the pool at the opposite end. This was business. She hated people who mixed pleasure with business, using every opportunity to turn a simple conversation into a flirtation.

And she'd really hate herself if she was the one doing it.

She slipped into her cover-up and flip-flops and walked slowly back to the cabin. *Face the truth, Jeannie. It's finally happened.* Her sister had said that one day it would. So had her brothers. And her parents had promised that the time would come when her heart would welcome a new love. A new life.

Until today Jeannie hadn't believed a word of it.

Of course, she couldn't do a thing about it. Why he'd probably laugh if he knew what she was thinking. Big joke. Lonely baby wrangler has the hots for sexy ad exec with adorable baby. It probably happened all the time.

Besides, wanting to go to bed with him was nothing like falling in love. This was just her hormones talking, plain and simple.

She unlocked the door to their cabin and stepped inside. Hunter stood in the front room. Their eyes met. Then her eyes roamed. He wore trousers, open at the waist, and nothing else.

No, he wouldn't laugh if he knew what she was thinking.

He'd hose her down.

She fled to the shower and locked the door behind her.

JEANNIE DIDN'T SEE Hunter again until dinnertime.

"I grabbed something to eat with the Captain," he said, shrugging off his jacket and loosening his tie. "I'll take over with Daisy. You might as well enjoy the trip."

"Wonderful!" Jeannie forced a bright smile. "Let me change and I'm out of here."

"Better move it," Hunter said. "Last seating's in ten minutes."

The drop-dead cocktail dress greeted her when she slid open the closet door. Not tonight, she thought. She stripped off her shorts and T-shirt and donned a short red tank dress. Big silver earrings and a cuff bracelet and she was ready.

"See you later," she said, heading for the door.

He and Daisy were sitting on the floor rolling a bright yellow ball back and forth.

Hunter looked up. "Have fun."

She hesitated. "I'll be back early."

He offered a smile. "Don't rush on our account. Enjoy yourself."

RIGHT, thought Hunter as she closed the door behind her. Enjoy yourself. Have a great time.

He got to his feet and stormed around the little drawing room.

He'd seen the way the crew members scoped out the females on board. If you were soprano and clean shaven, you were fair game. Jeannie would be a tasty morsel for the hungry hordes.

"Animals," he muttered as Daisy watched him with rapt curiosity. Wouldn't you think a woman should be able to eat dinner in peace without having to deal with men on the make?

But hey—it wasn't any of his business. She was single and over twenty-one. She could do whatever she wanted as long as she was there for Daisy in the morning.

"You're not going to date until you're thirty," he said to Daisy. "In fact, you might become a nun."

Daisy laughed and waved her ring of plastic keys in the air.

"Smart girl," he said, laughing along with the baby. "You know sound advice when you hear it."

The change in Daisy these past eight months had been amazing. She'd changed from the helpless, formless infant he'd brought back from Tokyo into a little person with a real personality and, he noted with amazement, the beginning of a sense of humor.

Not that he had much to do with any of those changes. He suspected they would have happened right on schedule whether or not he'd been around to see them happening. Parents made a big mistake when they took credit for little Johnny's first step, first word, first everything—it was all part of the process that nature had laid out a millenium or two ago.

The evening passed slowly. He bathed Daisy and put her to bed, sitting a while with her until she fell asleep. The crib was set perpendicular to Jeannie's bed and he sat on the edge of the narrow mattress. It seemed to him that the faint scent of her perfume was everywhere, not overpowering but just enough to tantalize. To send his imagination down pathways he'd be better off avoiding.

He wondered what she was doing then grimaced at the thought. It was none of his business if she let herself be seduced under the stars by some guy in an expensive suit. It was the 90s, wasn't it? Sex might be safer, but that didn't mean it was nonexistent.

Quietly he rose from the bed, took a quick glance at Daisy, then satisfied that she was sleeping soundly, walked into the sitting room. Tilting his head, he listened as footsteps approached the stateroom door.

"Really, Eddie, I appreciate the offer but I simply can't." Jeannie's voice, her tone brisk and friendly, was unmistakable.

"What's stopping you?" came a male voice. "You said you're not married."

"That's right, I'm not married."

Hunter's hands clenched into fists at his side. If that sonofabitch so much as reached for Jeannie, he would—

"Then what's the deal? It's only ten o'clock. The night's young. They've got a great band in the disco. I'll bet you're a terrific dancer."

"Two left feet. It runs in my family. My parents couldn't even dance at their own wedding."

"I'll teach you."

"Not tonight, thanks."

"I might not be available tomorrow night."

"I'll take my chances," said Jeannie.

Hunter grinned. *Good going, Ross. You put that bozo in his place.*

Guys like that gave men a bad rap. In his opinion they should be put on an ice floe and set adrift off the coast of Antarctica.

Jeannie's key scratched in the lock and he took up his position, sprawled across the little sofa.

"Back so soon?" He feigned a yawn.

"Mmmph," said Jeannie.

"How was dinner?"

"Food, 10. Companion, 0."

"Sorry." He tried to sound as if he meant it. "I thought there were some pretty nice people on board."

"There are," said Jeannie. "Eddie wasn't one of them."

"Eddie?"

She kicked off her heels and glared at him as she sank into a mini version of a Queen Anne chair. "Oh, don't give me that innocent look, Hunter. You heard every single word we said out there."

He felt like a kid caught peeping through a keyhole. "How'd you know?"

She rolled her eyes and pointed to the floor near the door. "The light spilled under the door into the corridor." She paused for effect. "At least it does when you aren't standing there."

"The guy was a jerk," Hunter said. "You were right to dump him."

She ran her fingers through her short cap of silky black hair. Did she have any idea how sexy she looked when she did that? "I don't recall asking you," she said.

"A lot of hormones on the loose on this ship. You'd better watch yourself."

She laughed out loud. "I'll keep that in mind. Don't worry, Hunter," she said, rising to her feet. He watched, rapt as her slinky red dress settled itself north of her knees. "I won't forget why I'm here. You have work to do. I'm here to give you the time to do it."

He stood up and faced her. "Look, I didn't mean it the way it sounded, Jeannie."

She glanced toward the porthole, at the moonlit sea shimmering beyond the glass, then back again at him. He wished he knew what she was thinking.

"Is Daisy asleep?" she asked.

That wasn't what he'd been expecting. "Out like a light. The sea air agrees with her."

She moved toward the door to the room she shared with the baby. "I guess I'll turn in."

"It's been a long day," he said.

She gave him her first real smile of the evening. "And Daisy's bound to wake up at the crack of dawn."

"Earlier," he said, relaxing. "My girl hits the ground running."

"Good night, Hunter," she said, turning away. "Sleep well."

NEITHER of them did.

The rocking of the ship kept him awake. At least that's what he told himself as he lay in his narrow bed and stared up at the ceiling. It had nothing to do with Jeannie. Nothing at all.

He didn't give a damn about her glossy black hair or sapphire-blue eyes. The fact that she had the kind of sexy little body that was made for Spandex didn't matter. Her throaty laugh...her walk—

Oh, hell.

So what if a few fantasies fired their way across his inner landscape?

They didn't mean a thing.

JEANNIE BLAMED IT ON her mattress. How could anyone sleep on a giant marshmallow? Certainly her sleeplessness had nothing to do with the fact that Hunter lay in his bed on the other side of the wall.

Naked.

She turned on her side and punched her pillow. Hard. He wasn't the kind to sleep in pajamas. Probably he didn't own a pair. Besides, with a body like his, why would he cover it up? She buried her face in the pillow, wishing away the images burning her brain cells. He probably spent half his time staring in the mirror at his own magnificence. She hated men who were in love with their own reflections.

Not even that was enough to cool her imagination.

In truth she knew there was more to Hunter Phillips than his glossy package would indicate. Selfishness was part and parcel of modern life. Not many men would give up their independence in order to raise a newborn baby. Fewer still would do so with the same degree of love and commitment as Hunter.

You couldn't fake something like that. Maybe he was reluctant to think of Daisy as his daughter, but that didn't change the fact that he loved her in the way a baby needed to be loved. People talked a lot about quality time, but when you're eight months old, you need someone to hug you and rock you to sleep. As far as she could tell, Hunter had been there to do exactly that for Daisy.

Hunter was nothing like Dan. There was an edge to Hunter that she had never seen in her late husband. Hunter was blatantly ambitious, aggressive, inclined to grab what he wanted, consequences be damned. She'd been watching him work on this trip and seen the way he pushed his agenda, driving forward in pursuit of his goal.

That type of man had never appealed to her before, but she found herself wondering how it would feel to be the goal he was pursuing.

Twice that night she got up to look at Daisy. She worked with babies every day. You would think she'd be immune to their charms. But how could she have forgotten the sweet smell of a sleeping child or the soft sounds they made as their dreams carried them away. It was all part of the same whole.

She'd forgotten so much...pushed so many feelings away, just beyond reach. The dark longing for someone to hold her through the night. She missed sex and all it encompassed, it was true, but tenderness? Dear God, there was no substitute for someone who cared that you were happy at the end of a long day.

HUNTER WOKE UP early the next morning, feeling disoriented. He was accustomed to the rumble of garbage trucks, the blare of taxis, the city's incessant roar. The absence of sound struck him as slightly strange. He washed and dressed quickly, half expecting to hear Daisy's familiar morning wail but even that was absent.

He glanced at the clock. Okay, he was about an hour ahead of schedule, but you'd think he'd hear *something* from the other room. Strange surroundings, strange roommate—the poor kid must be wondering what the hell was going on.

He rapped lightly on the door to Jeannie's room. No answer. He rapped again. Still no answer. Babysitters weren't supposed to sleep like the dead.

Slowly he pushed open the door. The room was dark. The curtains were drawn across the porthole. Sure enough, Daisy was wide-awake, happily playing with her toes. Back home she'd be wailing at the top of her lungs, demanding instant attention. Here she was content to smile up at the ceiling.

He bent over the crib and scooped her up into his arms. To his surprise her diaper seemed dry. Definitely not your average morning. Turning, he glanced toward the bed pushed up against the wall. He'd told himself he wasn't going to look over at Jeannie, but the pull was undeniable.

Not that there was anything to see. He took a step closer to the bed. The only clue that she was even in there was the silky cap of black hair peeking out from the covers. She stirred slightly, more a rustle of sheets than actual movement, but it was enough to send him heading for the door.

JEANNIE AWOKE slowly. She lay still, waiting for the familiar sounds of New York City to assail her. Instead she heard the ocean, the hum of the ship's engines, and—

She sat up straight in bed, heart pounding.

Daisy!

There wasn't a sound from the crib. No soft breathing or happy gurgling or even downright crying. Nothing.

She tossed back the covers and leaped from the bed.

"Daisy! Are you—"

The crib was empty.

She stared down at it. The one thing she knew with certainty was that the baby didn't climb out on her own and stroll down to the dining room for breakfast.

Hunter, she thought indignantly. He must have walked right into her room and fetched Daisy from her crib. Of course that wasn't a crime. Daisy was his daughter. He could fetch her anytime he wanted to.

But this was her *bedroom!* He had no business barging into her bedroom like that, not unless Daisy had been crying or—

"Oh, God," she breathed. What if Daisy had been crying and she'd slept right through it? She wouldn't have imagined it possible, but what other explanation could there possibly be.

She burst into the drawing room, heart pounding with fear. "Hunter! Is she okay? Where is—"

She stopped dead in her tracks.

"About time," said Hunter, looking up from feeding Daisy. "I ordered a little of everything, but it's first come, first served."

The table was set with snowy-white linens and piled high with platters of toasted bagels, flaky croissants, and mounds of fluffy scrambled eggs. A crystal goblet filled with freshly squeezed orange juice waited for her—and a glorious pot of rich, strong coffee.

Daisy was happily seated in a high chair, making a mess of her food.

"Breakfast," he said, gesturing toward the tiny Queen Anne chair pulled up to the rolling cart. "I figured we should all have at least one meal together on this trip.'' He pointed to a bowl of hot cereal with pureed strawberries. ''Even something special for Daisy.''

Jeannie pushed her hair off her forehead. ''She's okay?''

''Of course she's okay.''

First she felt relief. Then: ''How dare you come into my room without my permission!''

His jaw dropped. If she hadn't been so embarrassed, she would have laughed.

''You were sleeping. I wanted to spend time with Daisy.''

A likely story. ''Why didn't you knock?''

''I did,'' he said. ''Twice.''

Her face flamed. Now she sounded like a righteous incompetent. What a wonderful combination. ''You should have knocked harder.''

''That would have defeated the purpose, Jeannie. I didn't want to wake you up.''

''I'm supposed to wake up,'' she said. ''Daisy's my responsibility.'' She paused. ''Besides, I deserve my privacy.''

''I didn't see anything, if that's what you're worried about.'' The twinkle in his eyes was unmistakable. ''You had the covers pulled up to your eyeballs.'' He flashed her a downright wicked grin. ''Not like right now.''

She glanced down and was horrified to see she was standing there in front of him in an oversize pink

T-shirt and little else. "Oh, my God!" Turning, she fled to her room as Hunter burst into laughter.

IT WAS EITHER LAUGH or cry, Hunter thought as Jeannie disappeared in a blur of very appealing female flesh. Seeing her in a bathing suit had been tough enough on his self-control; seeing her in that shorty nightshirt was cruel and inhuman punishment.

Even though he'd seen more of her body yesterday by the swimming pool, the impact had been softened by the circumstances. No such luck this morning. Seeing her rosy from sleep with her defenses down had lent an intimacy to the situation that had no business being there.

"Forget it," he said out loud. Forget the supple line of her legs. Forget the faint scent of her skin that lingered in the air. Forget the way she looked more beautiful with her face scrubbed bare and her hair tousled than most women looked after a day in the salon.

"Daah?" Daisy pounded on his arm with her chubby fist.

"Sorry," he said, shaking away the disturbing thoughts. "Let's get back to breakfast."

JEANNIE EMERGED from her room a few minutes later and sat down to breakfast.

Hunter finished feeding Daisy while Jeannie ate, then she took over so he could devour a bagel. But there was something else at work, an awareness of each other as a man and a woman that made each movement into something more.

Their hands brushed when they reached for the cream cheese at the same time. He caught the faint scent of her perfume and thought of warm summer evenings, making love beneath the stars. She breathed in the tang of soap and wondered if his skin was still warm from his morning shower.

When she bent down to retrieve Daisy's spoon, the shadow between her breasts sent his blood racing south. Dangerous business, wanting a woman who didn't want you.

"Do you have a lot of meetings?" Jeannie asked.

"Straight through until dinner," said Hunter.

"So we won't see you again today?"

"Probably not."

"You're working awfully hard."

"That's why they sent me." He watched, mesmerized by the sight of her breasts rising and falling beneath the thin cotton of her T-shirt. "I'm here to work. Nothing else."

Hold that thought.

HUNTER HAD TO WORK through dinner. "I'll keep Daisy with me," he said, not looking up from the mountain of paper scattered from one end of the cabin to the other. "You go and have fun."

"Are you sure you don't want anything?"

He looked up from his stack of papers. She wore a silky dress in a vivid shade of turquoise. The fact that it stopped a handful of inches above her knees wasn't lost on him. "If you stumbled across a BLT, I wouldn't complain."

"I'll see what I can do."

She closed the door behind her. Hunter reached for the glass of ice water on the table and debated the wisdom of dumping it on his head.

She looked too sexy for his own good.

And not only was she great to look at, but she was down-to-earth, fun to be around, and terrific with kids.

If she knew he was alive, he'd be in big trouble.

THE MAIN BALLROOM of the *Star of the Atlantic* was ablaze with light. Huge crystal chandeliers twinkled overhead. Tuxedo-clad waiters bearing champagne circulated among the crowd. The music was lush. The atmosphere heady with perfume and expectations.

Jeannie gave it her best shot. She danced with those who asked her. She made frothy conversation with the same people she'd laughed with at lunchtime.

But it was no use.

She had just one thing on her mind.

You're an idiot, she told herself. There she was in the middle of the ocean, on one of the most glamorous cruise ships in the world, and all she could think of was finding Hunter a BLT.

You're a sap…a total moron!

The man could move mountains. She had no doubt he could find his own sandwich. She was there to care for Daisy, not Daisy's daddy.

That morning she'd caught a glimpse of Hunter deep in conversation with a pair of stern-looking businessmen. He was all sharp edges and intensity, that single-minded determination propelling him forward with the same inevitability of the tides. There was nothing comfortable or safe about him.

With Daisy he was approachable, loving, the kind of guy you could sit with at the kitchen table over pizza.

But the man she'd seen that morning was hard-driving, sophisticated, the kind of man who took what he wanted, no matter the cost.

Not her kind of man at all. There were scores of interesting people on board—and many men just as gorgeous as Hunter Phillips. Wasn't it just her luck that the most interesting of them all was the one who didn't know she was alive?

Still he was working so hard, she thought, and he had managed to surprise her with that beautiful breakfast.

What would it hurt to do something nice for him?

HUNTER WAS DROWNING in a sea of half-written proposals when Jeannie returned to the cabin.

"I couldn't find a BLT," she said in a matter-of-fact fashion, "but how does tuna on rye sound?"

He looked up from his work. Damn it. She still looked great. "Tuna sounds fine," he said, glancing around. "Where is it?" Images of dinner-for-two sprang to life. Tuna wasn't chateaubriand but it was a good place to start. Besides, it meant she didn't have plans for the rest of the evening.

"In the lounge," she said, heading for the door. "Ask for Conrad. He'll set you up."

COWARD, thought Jeannie as the door closed behind her. *You didn't have the guts to be alone with him.*

LIAR, thought Hunter, as he headed toward the lounge. *You don't even want the damn sandwich anymore.*
He wanted to be with her.

Chapter Five

Jeannie woke before dawn. She lay in bed, listening to the sound of Daisy's even breathing and waiting for Hunter to knock on the door.

And he was going to. Her feminine intuition, which had been silent the past few years, told her so. There weren't many things in life of which she was sure, but this was one of them. Any minute he was going to pop up at her door to fetch Daisy—and maybe shoot a quick glance in her direction, as well?

The thought was enough to make her laugh out loud. He hadn't given the slightest indication that he saw her as anything but Daisy's baby-sitter and there was no reason to think that situation was going to change.

You don't have to lie here like an idiot, waiting for him, Ross. Why don't you get up, get dressed, and have Daisy waiting for him when he shows up?

It was the logical thing to do. And it would certainly bypass the inevitable discomfort they would both feel when he stepped into the room.

But she didn't. She lay there, savoring the feeling of being connected to the world in a way she hadn't been in a long, long time. She was important. Both to Daisy and to Hunter. It felt better than she'd remembered.

Meeting Hunter and his little girl had awakened in her a sense of wonder that made life seem to glow with promise.

Of course, being around Hunter had certain built-in drawbacks but she was reasonably certain she was doing a good job of concealing the attraction she felt toward him. She'd rather die than let him know she was mooning over him like a lovesick schoolgirl.

"Jeannie." She heard Hunter's voice from the other side of the doorway. "You awake?"

She cleared her throat. "Y-yes."

"Can I come in and get Daisy?"

Heat rose from the center of her body, over her breasts, her throat. "Come in."

The door squeaked open. He stood for a moment in the doorway, his broad frame silhouetted by the lights in the drawing room. He wore a pair of running shorts and a T-shirt and he looked aggressively male. She became extremely aware of the fact that beneath the covers she wore a lacy teddy. She'd never slept in a lacy teddy before last night. She didn't care to consider why she'd chosen to do so.

"Come on, Daisy," he said, leaning over the crib. "Rise and shine."

Her breath caught as he bent low to reach for Daisy. His legs were powerfully muscled, moving nicely up to a narrow waist and broad chest. It was a wonder someone at C V & S hadn't asked him to spend time on the other side of the camera.

"Breakfast's on its way up," he said, turning back to her with a sleepy Daisy curled against his chest. "The bathroom's yours."

"Great."

He stood there in the doorway, an absolutely gorgeous male specimen with an equally gorgeous baby in his arms. He met her eyes. She let herself be held by his gaze. Tension shimmered in the air between them, glittering like a golden thread of promise.

"Better hurry," he said. "Don't want the coffee to get cold."

So much for romance.

THE THING TO DO was get out of there.

Hunter had it all planned.

The second Jeannie sat down to breakfast, he intended to grab a bagel and head for the hills.

Something was happening between them, something he didn't have the time nor the energy to deal with. Back in that bedroom, all he'd wanted to do was drag her from that bed, pull her body up against his, and kiss her until he didn't want to kiss her anymore.

Unfortunately, however, this was the 90s and enlightened men didn't do things like that unless they enjoyed lawsuits and exposés on *Donahue* and *Oprah Winfrey.*

A few minutes later she sat down opposite him. He

was burning with lust; she looked as cool as the ocean breeze.

"If I keep eating like this, I'll be too big to fit through the doorways," she said, reaching for a croissant. "Better hurry, Hunter, before I devour everything that isn't nailed down."

He polished off a cup of coffee. "Hate to eat and run," he said, "but I have a meeting in five minutes, then two more meetings after that."

"I understand," said Jeannie. "This *is* a business trip, after all."

If only he could remember that....

LATER THAT MORNING she saw Hunter talking to a woman she assumed was a showgirl from the Vegas-style revue and it occurred to her there was such a thing as being too tall and leggy and blond.

It also occurred to her that it didn't look much like business. Apparently Hunter could find a few spare moments for flirtation when he was motivated enough.

Of course he could do what he wanted with his time. She was the employee. He certainly didn't have to explain himself to her. Just because she was enmeshed in romantic daydreams, was no reason to assume he gave her more than a second thought.

If he wanted to have lunch with a blonde and dinner with a redhead, he certainly didn't have to ask her permission.

"Life is very complicated," she said to Daisy as they reclined on the deck chair and watched Hunter.

"Daah?" Daisy waved her hands in the air and strained toward Hunter.

"Yes, that's Daddy," Jeannie said, playing patty cake with the baby's hands. "Making a fool of himself over a woman half his age."

Another woman joined Hunter and the blonde. A redhead. Buzzes of conversation drifted across the deck toward Jeannie. "Probably talking about quantum physics," she said with a sniff that Daisy found quite amusing. *Tough job, Phillips. Don't wear yourself out.*

The group commandeered a table near the pool and continued their animated conversation sitting down. Nice work if you could get it.

"Come on, Daisy," she said. "It's time for lunch."

"Exactly what I was going to say."

She squinted up into the sunshine at an impressive male physique. "Excuse me?"

"Tim Reeves," he said, extending a hand. "Glad to see you're alone."

"Jeannie Ross." She gestured toward Daisy. "And I wouldn't say I'm alone."

"Great kid," he said, hunkering down next to them. "What I meant was—"

"I know what you meant," said Jeannie. "You're a friend of Eddie's, aren't you?" Her favorite obnoxious football player from the other night.

"Don't hold it against me." He flashed her a smile. "I'm a lot nicer."

Thank heaven for sunglasses. She cast a glance toward Hunter. To her delight, he was scowling in her direction.

She chatted with Tim for a few minutes, relishing the fact that Hunter apparently found it impossible to tear his eyes away from the touching scene.

HUNTER EXCUSED HIMSELF from the table where he'd been talking print-ad space with two of the cruise line's junior executives.

"We'll continue this at the afternoon presentation," he said, then headed straight for Jeannie and that muscle brain who was making an obvious play for her. Look at the way the bozo was fawning all over Daisy. Talk about being blatant....

"Isn't it time for Daisy's lunch?" he asked without preamble.

Those damn sunglasses of Jeannie's hid her expression, which was probably a good thing. He had the distinct feeling she didn't appreciate the interruption.

"Tim Reeves," said the bozo, extending his paw. "And you're—?"

"Phillips." He squeezed the guy's hand hard. The bozo didn't blink. He turned toward Jeannie. "Lunchtime," he said, ignoring the predator at his side.

"Just what Tim and I were discussing." She paused, watching him through those damn sunglasses. If she thought he was going to volunteer to free her to have lunch with that clown—

"Great to meet you, Reeves," he said, placing a

hand under Jeannie's elbow and steering her toward the indoor promenade. "Enjoy your lunch."

To her credit, she kept her own counsel until they reached the cabin, but then all hell broke loose.

"Of all the insufferably arrogant, high-handed things to do, that takes the cake. What on earth did you think you were doing?"

"I know his type," he said through clenched teeth.

"You *are* his type," she retorted. "Bullheaded, hot tempered—" She stopped.

"Go ahead. Say whatever you were going to say."

She tossed her sunglasses down on top of the bar and stormed into her bedroom with Daisy.

He was right behind her.

"We're not through talking."

"Want to bet?" She placed Daisy in the middle of the bed and unfastened her diaper. She winced, then disposed of it.

He handed her a fresh one.

"Thanks," she muttered, cleaning Daisy's bottom with practiced motions.

"Look," he began, "maybe I overreacted back there."

She looked up at him, brows lifted, then back down at Daisy. "No argument here."

"He's a friend of that creep you had trouble with that night. I didn't want to see you have—" *Have what?* he thought. Have a good time with him?

Have dinner?

An affair?

Gambling was legal beyond the three-mile limit. Good thing murder wasn't. Eddie and Tim would be history.

JEANNIE'S HEART was pounding so furiously she had to take a series of deep breaths to calm herself down. Part of it was justifiable anger over his display of male territoriality, but an equal part was pure exhilaration.

He was jealous.

Unfounded.

Illogical.

But true.

Some things a woman just knew. It was in the set of his jaw, the way his hands were clenched into fists at his side, the deep rumble of his voice.

She fastened Daisy's diaper then lifted her up. She nuzzled the baby's neck then handed her to Hunter.

"I want to change for lunch," she said blithely. "Tim will be waiting."

Hunter struggled with his temper. "I thought we could eat together."

"I thought you had a meeting."

"I do. My usual meeting after lunch."

"I wish I'd known."

"You could cancel your date with Jim."

"Tim," she said. "And no, I couldn't." She reminded herself that this wasn't real life they were talking about here. She didn't owe Hunter anything beyond taking good care of his little girl. Once they returned to New York City, he'd go his way and she'd go hers. There was nothing between them except a business agreement.

"My meeting's at two," he said, his tone brusque.

"Fine," she said, her tone equally clipped. "I'll be back in plenty of time."

"Good," he said.

"Great," she said, heading for the door.

HUNTER LISTENED to Jeannie's footsteps disappearing down the hallway.

"Go to work," he said out loud. "That's why you're here."

It seemed as if everything was conspiring to pull him away from his goal. For eight months he'd been mired on the Daddy Track at work. Two steps forward, three back. That wasn't how great careers were made. Grantham had set up this trip to be Hunter's personal Waterloo. One screwup and Grantham would have all the ammunition he needed to send Hunter's butt straight to the Unemployment Office.

How the hell had his life degenerated into such a pitiful mess, he wondered. He'd lived without romance this long, he could live without it a while longer. He was confusing convenience with chemistry, that was all. Jeannie was there to take care of Daisy, not provide inspiration for his sexual imagination.

THE PREDINNER MEETING was a success. So was the dinner.

The after-dinner meeting, however, turned out to

be more social than constructive and Hunter found himself looking for a way out.

"You're a great dancer, Hunter." Sarah, an executive for the cruise line, tilted her head back and met his eyes. "You must get a lot of practice."

He looked at her blankly. "Did I miss something? I thought we were discussing TV ad time."

"I think we've pretty well covered the TV issue," said Sarah. "Serious conversations are anathema on cruise ships."

She was flirting. No doubt about it. The signals were clear, even to Hunter.

"So you think we've finished up for the night?"

"Absolutely," said Sarah.

The song ended. Hunter escorted Sarah back to the table they'd shared with other cruise line execs.

"I'm calling it a night," he said to the group at large. "I have some more paperwork to catch up on before the morning meeting." *Good going, Phillips,* he thought even as he uttered the words. *You get them eating out of the palm of your hand and then you take a hike.* He'd never get back in the fast lane this way.

"Stay," urged one of the cruise ship's top brass. "You've done enough hard work. How can you sell a cruise ship when you haven't experienced any of the fun?"

Good question. "Wish I could hang around," said Hunter, "but I'll have to take a rain check."

With that he shook hands all around then made his exit.

The ship was rocking badly and he negotiated his

way through the lounge by grabbing ahold of chair backs and any stationary objects he could find.

"Slow down, sailor!" called out an inebriated man in a bow tie. "You're making me dizzy."

Hunter didn't slow down. It was nearing midnight and he wanted to get back to the cabin in time to patch over the rough spot he and Jeannie had experienced that afternoon. Besides, he missed Daisy.

He unlocked the door and stepped inside the drawing room. A tiny lamp burned on the tiny desk, but other than that, all was still. And quiet.

"Damn," he muttered, tossing his room key down on the minisofa. He considered knocking on her bedroom door but that would only wake up Daisy and defeat his purpose entirely.

He yanked off his tie then helped himself to a tumbler of Scotch. In some ways it might have been easier if he'd schlepped Daisy to all the meetings himself and saved himself the complications he'd found with Jeannie.

Of course he hadn't figured there would *be* any complications when he'd put the idea to her the night they'd shared the pastrami sandwiches. The whole thing had seemed pretty straightforward.

Showed how much he knew about life.

Watching her with Daisy called up all sorts of feelings inside him. Hallmark Card feelings. Nothing like he'd ever felt before—or even imagined, for that matter.

And tangled up in that mess of hearth and home

was a very real, very fiery attraction that was making it hard for him to remember this trip was work and not play.

EARLY SUNDAY morning the *Star of the Atlantic* executed a slow and lazy loop, then headed back toward New York.

Despite herself, Jeannie supposed it wasn't a moment too soon. She and Hunter had never recovered that easy camaraderie they'd shared at the beginning. Not that there hadn't been some fiery sparks of temper at the start. Funny thing, their bursts of temper hadn't really been the problem.

It was their growing awareness of each other that was making things difficult.

"Speak for yourself," she muttered as she fed Daisy her breakfast cereal and nursed her own cup of coffee. Just because she was mooning around like a starry-eyed schoolgirl was no reason to think her feelings were reciprocated.

Obviously they weren't. The man was doing his level best to keep his distance. In the past twenty-four hours they'd barely seen each other except to say hello and pass on information about Daisy.

After breakfast she dressed Daisy in an adorable bright blue romper outfit with a matching headband then donned skorts and a T-shirt. They watched a shuffleboard match, dangled their bare feet in the outdoor swimming pool, watched the clouds drifting overhead in kaleidoscopic patterns.

Lunch came and went without a sign of Hunter anywhere. She knew he'd been sent on this cruise with expectations of failure. Bagging the cruise line's account would go a long way toward cementing his position at C V & S. And she wanted that for him.

Daisy's eyes drooped not long after lunch. Jeannie excused herself to put the baby down for a nap. In truth she'd half expected to find Hunter in their cabin with his briefcase and papers strewn from stem to stern.

The cabin looked as immaculate as her apartment—and every bit as lonely. She hated that untouched look and she set about rumpling pillows and generally mussing things up the best she could.

She put Daisy down in her crib then rattled around the suite, at loose ends. She flipped on the ship's radio, heard a lushly romantic ballad, then switched it off. She gazed out the porthole but was too short to see anything but sky.

She glanced at the clock. A little after two. Five hours until the Captain's Farewell Dinner.

Her spirits lifted. *Everyone* attended that dinner, crew and passengers alike. Hunter had made sure even Daisy had a frilly velvet-and-lace outfit packed for the occasion and he and Jeannie had spent an agreeable time debating the wisdom of pablum at a six-course formal dinner.

She took her drop-dead gorgeous black cocktail dress from the closet and hung it on the door.

"Tonight or never," she said out loud with a glance toward the sleeping baby. There might be nothing between her and Hunter, but that didn't mean she couldn't look smashing.

She'd take a leisurely bubble bath while Daisy slep and Hunter was out doing whatever it was he did She'd shave her legs and cream her face and condi tion her hair until it shone like black satin. She'd spend ages on her makeup, doing up her eyes with all the tricks she hadn't had time for in far too long

Then she'd admire herself in the mirror and wish with all her heart that she didn't feel so alone.

BOTH JEANNIE and Daisy were dressed and ready by six-thirty. Daisy looked absolutely precious in her velvet-and-lace outfit with her soft cloud of blond fluff drifting over her velvet headband. Jeannie didn' look so bad herself.

6:40. There was no sign of Hunter.

Jeannie paced the drawing room. Four steps thi way. Four steps that way. Daisy amused herself with her set of plastic keys.

6:45.

6:50.

"Damn you, Hunter," she muttered under he breath so Daisy wouldn't hear.

It just wasn't fair! Her skin was soft, she wasn' PMSing, and it was a good hair day. The odds of al three things occurring simultaneously again in he lifetime were right up there with being struck by meteorite.

7:00.

Still no sign of Hunter. She picked up Daisy and the two of them paced the room.

"Were we supposed to meet your daddy in the dining room?"

Daisy looked at her, eyes wide.

By 7:15 Jeannie was growing apprehensive. Maybe something had happened to him. Maybe his appendix had burst or he'd fallen overboard or—

Or maybe he was standing in the doorway looking exhausted and repentant.

"Hunter!" She ran to him, Daisy in tow. "I was so worried!"

His eyes widened slightly in surprise, the way Daisy's did when something new and wonderful caught her attention. There was a definite family resemblance. "My presentation hit a land mine," he said, putting down his briefcase and taking Daisy in his arms for a hug. "Sorry."

"You can't go to the Captain's Party?"

He shook his head. "I have an hour to regroup and come up with something new."

To her horror tears welled up and she quickly turned away.

"No reason you should miss it," he said. "I'll watch Daisy."

"How can you watch Daisy when you have to work?"

"I've been doing it for eight months now, Jeannie. I'll manage."

She reached for the child. "No," she said, voice firm. "You're paying me so you can do your job. She'll come with me." By the time he had her fed, his hour would be up. "What about your dinner?"

He brushed that aside. ''I'll worry about that later.'' He gestured toward his briefcase. ''I tossed a bag of chips in there. That'll hold me.''

She started toward the door, feeling sad, lonely, and generally miserable.

''Jeannie?''

She turned around. ''Yes?''

''You look great.''

THIS TIME the presentation was a success. The big guns congratulated him. Sarah offered her help on second-phase planning. Everyone had something they wanted to add to the mix.

Maybe he was finally hitting his stride again after his long dry spell. He felt as if he was popping on all cylinders. The ideas were coming as fast as he could write them down—and they were good ideas, too, quick and sharp and bound to sell a million widgets to people who never even knew they needed one.

He fielded questions like a Hall of Famer and when it was finally his turn at bat he hit one right out of the park.

He couldn't wait to get back to the cabin and tell Jeannie. None of this would have been possible without her help. If she hadn't been there to care for Daisy, he would have gone 0-for-4 in a puff of baby powder.

It was nearly eight o'clock when he returned to the cabin. Jeannie and Daisy were nowhere to be found. He couldn't blame them. He'd told her to enjoy dinner and she was probably doing so. Still, he was disappointed.

Tired and disappointed.

He decided on a quick shower to revive himself. Fumbling in the amenities basket for some soap, he was startled to find a plastic cap, a sewing kit, and a condom discreetly wrapped and labeled. Talk about hospitality....

The shower over, he felt upbeat and optimistic and hungry.

It occurred to him that even though the Captain's Farewell Dinner was over, it wouldn't hurt to stroll around and check things out. And if he happened to bump into Jeannie and Daisy—well, it was a small world.

As it turned out, he didn't have far to look. He bumped into Jeannie and his little girl near the elevator.

Daisy looked adorable in her blue velvet dress with the white collar and matching headband. Jeannie's sparkly black dress clung to her breasts and hips in an extremely provocative fashion. Not that it was his business, but he was glad Daisy was with her. With a dress like Jeannie was almost wearing, she probably needed an armed guard to keep the bozos away.

"Hunter!" Her surprise was evident. He wouldn't have minded if she looked happier to see him. "Did you finish your presentation?"

He grabbed Daisy and sat her on his shoulders. "Not only finished it, but managed to push it through."

"You cinched the deal?"

"Nailed it," he said with a wide grin.

Impulsively she threw her arms around him. "That's terrific! You worked so hard to make it happen."

He felt her touch everywhere—in places he'd forgotten about. She must have sensed his reaction because she backed away, patches of bright red staining her cheeks.

"I couldn't have done it without you, Jeannie. If you hadn't been here to watch Daisy I would've blown it just the way Grantham expected me to do."

"You would have found a way," she said, deeply pleased despite her words to the contrary.

"Still can't take a compliment, Ross?" He took her arm and headed for the elevator. "Come on. I need to find some food. Those chips were only an appetizer."

"Let's go back to the cabin."

"The cabin? There's nothing there. I'm ready to eat wallpaper, Jeannie. Let's—"

"The cabin," she repeated.

"I DON'T KNOW how you managed this," he said to Jeannie as the cabin steward wheeled in a cart piled high with food. It might not be seduction but it wasn't a bad second choice.

"All it took was a little persistence," she said, beaming at him from her perch on the sofa. "But you should know that, Hunter. You conjured up some wonderful breakfasts for us." Her strappy sandals rested on the floor. Her stockinged feet were tucked beneath her. Not panty hose, he thought. She was too sexy for panty hose.

"Is there anything else I can get for you?" the cabin steward asked.

Hunter looked at Jeannie and felt a rush of heat. "We're fine," he said. If being on fire was fine...

He disappeared to put Daisy down for the night.

Daisy expressed her disapproval loudly when he tried to put her sleeper on backward.

"Sorry," he mumbled, feeling like a jerk. "My mind's somewhere else tonight, Daisy."

He thought of Jeannie in her sexy black dress and a dark fire seemed to gather heat inside his body. He brushed Daisy's hair back with his hand then kissed her on top of her sweet-smelling head.

"Let's make a deal, Daisy," he said as she smiled up at him. "You sleep through the night tonight and I'll see to it you have ice cream tomorrow."

"Daah," she said, offering up her best toothless smile.

"That's yes in Russian," he said. "I'm going to hold you to it."

He tucked her in, shut off the light, then went back into the drawing room. Jeannie had switched on the cabin sound system and soft music gentled the air. She was curled up on the sofa, that lethal black dress sliding up around her thighs. She held a flute of champagne between her elegant fingers and he reached for his own glass on the end table. Instead of seeming cramped and tiny, the drawing room now seemed intimate.

"To your mission accomplished," she said.

He raised his own glass in salute. "To you."

Their eyes locked. Her hand shook as she brought the glass to her mouth. That shimmering sense of destiny she'd felt the first moment she saw him was all around her.

"Eat," she said. "The food's wonderful."

"No," he said, in a measured voice. "*You* are."

She placed her glass down on the end table. A few golden droplets spilled over the lip and onto the wood. Neither noticed. She felt as if she were standing in the eye of a storm with the wild winds all around her.

The only safe haven was in his arms.

He pushed back his chair and stood up.

She waited, scarcely breathing, as he crossed the room. The world had narrowed down to this moment.

And this man.

"Let's dance," he said.

She tilted her head. An old Johnny Mathis tune drifted toward her. The song was older than either of them. Its message was older than time.

She took his hand then rose to her feet. The pressure of his hand against the small of her back was incendiary. The way she fit against him was intoxicating.

The fact that they had found each other was nothing short of miraculous.

HER BREASTS were soft against his chest. He could feel her heart beating rapidly against his. With her forehead resting against his shoulder, he was ten feet tall.

Had music ever sounded as sweet?

Had dancing ever held such erotic promise?

Johnny Mathis segued into early Frank Sinatra. It didn't matter who was singing. He could only hear the way his blood pulsed through his veins.

He drew her closer to him. She was warm and pliant in his arms.

And he was ready.

"JEANNIE."

His voice reached into her heart. She raised her eyes.

"I'm going to kiss you, Jeannie."

"Of course you are." That kiss had been between them for days now. *For a lifetime.*

His hand moved from her shoulder, to the side of her neck, then trailed upward. He cupped her chin, running his thumb lightly across the line of her jaw. She had a fierce, primitive urge to draw his finger into her mouth and run her tongue across the sensitive ridge of flesh at his fingertip.

Slowly he lowered his head, bringing his mouth closer, closer to hers, until their lips met. He traced their fullness with his tongue, then swept along her teeth before entering her mouth. She gasped—it had been so long and the invasion was so hot, so sweet, the hunger so deep that it took her to a place she'd all but forgotten.

Teasing.

Tempting.

The kiss deepened until they were both left shaken and aching for more.

"The couch," said Jeannie, her fingers fumbling with the buttons on his shirt.

"Too small," he said, cupping her breasts. "Your room."

"Can't." She bared his chest then pressed her lips against his skin. "Daisy."

She started to suggest his room when he dropped to his knees in front of her. Involuntarily she stepped back, but he caught her behind the knees and drew her closer and closer until the heat of his breath burned against the tops of her thighs.

His hands were large and strong, his fingers questing. Inch by devastating inch his fingers moved their way under her skirt, sliding up the length of her stockings until he found the snaps of her black lace garter belt.

His laugh was low, thrilling.

She felt as if the world was spinning wildly on its axis and she gripped his shoulders in a desperate attempt to maintain her balance against this sensual onslaught. Her skirt was a froth of lace around her hips as his mouth found the soft skin of her thighs above the black silk stockings. She reached down to help him unsnap the garters but he caught her hand and held it fast.

"No," he said, his voice a delicious rumble. "Keep it on."

"But—"

Words died. He found her center with his mouth, his lips hot and wet against the fragile silk of her panties. She heard herself cry out when the fabric tore in his hands, that last barrier between them falling away as if it had never existed.

"Not yet," he whispered against her skin. "Not this way."

He rose to his feet and in the blink of an eye the rest of their clothing fell away from them and he reached for the packet he'd found near the tub earlier that evening.

He found himself staggered by her perfection. The round breasts with the taut, rosy peaks...the inward curve of her waist...the breathtaking outward flair of her hips.

She swayed gently on her feet and he pulled her up against him, lifting her until their eyes met. She gripped his shoulders, her nails teasing his skin. The question was in his eyes; the answer was in her soft sigh, the way she molded herself against him.

He leaned back against the wall, bracing his feet for balance. Slowly he lowered her until her body grazed his, sending shock waves of violent sensation tearing through his body. He wanted to bury himself in her but there was still a scrap of reason left and he hesitated, afraid he might hurt her with the intensity of his desire.

And then she smiled at him, a smile of infinite possibilities, and her eyes fluttered closed as she rocked slowly in his arms. She opened for him completely, wet and hot and ready, and his control finally snapped.

She welcomed him. She surrounded him. The rippling muscles of her sweet body sent wave after wave of pure sensation that took him to someplace he'd never been before.

When it was over, seconds or hours or aeons later, she fell limp in his arms, her heart thundering against him. His knees didn't feel any too steady.

With Jeannie still in his arms, he headed for his bedroom. "Fair warning," he said. "There's barely room enough in there for one person."

"Wonderful," Jeannie murmured, touching her tongue to his nipple.

He pushed open the door with his foot then carried her into the room.

They tumbled together to the bed.

"Oh," said Jeannie, finding herself between a wall and a built-in nightstand. "This *is* a small room."

With a lusty growl, he was on the bed next to her—

Then off again.

"Hunter!" A wild giggle escaped her lips. She leaned over the edge of the bed and looked down at him. "Did you hurt yourself?"

He was delayed but not deterred. Laughing, he climbed back into bed.

"This isn't going to be easy," he said as they tried to find a position.

"Most wonderful things aren't."

"I know," he said. "And you were wonderful before."

She ducked her head, torn between elation and a fierce rush of desire that all but stole her breath away. "I wish I were double-jointed."

He grinned as he shifted position. "So do I."

After some struggle, they hit upon a workable combination.

"You're a magician," she said as he gathered her in his arms.

"I'm determined."

They lay down together.

"I don't know about you," said Jeannie, "but I can't move."

"You're right," he said. "Neither can I."

He considered the situation then suggested an alternative.

"I don't know," said Jeannie, beginning to laugh. "It doesn't happen this way in the movies."

"You get one hundred takes in the movies." He shifted position. "Who knows what troubles Michelle Pfeiffer and Mel Gibson have on their own time."

She cupped his face in her hands. "Right now I wouldn't trade places with them for anything in this world."

"Even for a king-size bed?"

"Even for a king-size bed."

Inspiration is where you find it and that night Hunter and Jeannie were both inspired.

Chapter Six

There were no words for what happened between them that night.

At times they were awkward. At times, graceful.

They improvised and invented and always, *always,* there was pleasure.

And even when the last violent rush of passion had been spent, leaving them both exhausted and content, they lay together, still joined, hearts beating together, their breath mingling in the charged air.

"Are you okay?" he asked, his voice rumbling beneath her ear.

"Wonderful." Her cheek scraped deliciously against the thick mat of hair on his chest.

"I didn't—?"

"No," she said, kissing the tip of his chin. "You didn't."

"You felt so good, so tight." He stroked the inside of her thigh. "I couldn't hold back."

"I don't want you to hold back," she said fiercely.

"I want—" She stopped, listening. "Daisy's crying."

"Impossible. My girl has perfect timing. She'd never cry at a crucial moment like this."

She touched a finger to his lips. "Listen."

Sure enough. Daisy's wail grew louder.

With a rueful laugh Hunter eased himself away from Jeannie, then climbed out of bed.

"Wait until we're back home," he said, pulling on his pants. "I'm going to show you a night of real romance, not something out of a Marx Brothers' movie."

She smiled and lay back against the pillow, drinking in the smell of him...of *them*.

How could he possibly know that she didn't need flowers or candlelight or soft music to spell romance?

A man there beside you in the dark heart of the night. A baby who needed you. That painful, hopeful feeling pushing against the boundaries that had been set by fate and circumstance. All the wonders that came with real life.

It simply didn't get any better than this.

HUNTER TRIED everything he could think of to quell Daisy's tears but failed miserably. She wasn't wet or hungry or coming down with a fever.

"Sorry, Daise," he said as he scooped her up from the crib and held her against his bare chest. "I can't call for a cab, but this is the next best thing." He carried her, still crying, from the room and walked her from one side of the tiny drawing room to the other. Her cries were pitiful and his chest was quickly damp with her tears.

Every time he thought he was coming close to getting the hang of caring for her, Daisy threw him one of these curveballs that he found impossible to catch.

"A lullaby," he said, sitting down on the tiny sofa. In the old days, lullabies worked wonders. "Okay, Daisy," he said. "Here goes."

"What on earth is that racket?" Jeannie, clad in one of his shirts, appeared in the doorway a few moments later. "It sounded like nails on a blackboard."

He shot her a look. "I was singing."

"Oh, that's what you call it," said Jeannie, laughing. "Then why is the poor baby crying louder than she was before?"

"I don't know," he said, feeling about as useful as a dead battery. "I can't figure it out."

"I can," said Jeannie. "I'll bet she's cutting a tooth."

He tried to peek inside Daisy's tiny mouth but she only wailed louder. "Does she feel as bad as she sounds?" he asked, feeling more helpless than he had since the day Daisy was born.

"Afraid so." She held out her arms for the baby who was more than happy to wail in Jeannie's ear as well as his own.

A myriad emotions, all of them foreign, played themselves out inside Hunter as he watched the woman he had just made love to care for his baby girl. The transition from raw passion to tenderness was swift and sudden, but somehow he felt as if it were all part of the same wonderful whole.

She spoke low to Daisy, her voice soothing and almost hypnotic, and before long the baby's fair head dropped against Jeannie's shoulder. *This isn't about a job,* he thought as Jeannie walked up and down the length of the room. No one could fake the very real communication the woman and child shared.

Or the deep sense of coming home that grew inside his heart with each minute that passed.

THE SHIP DOCKED a little after ten in the morning. Daisy had finally fallen asleep a few hours earlier and Hunter and Jeannie had tiptoed around the suite, packing up their things for debarkation.

Instead of complicating matters, making love had freed Hunter and Jeannie to be their true selves for the first time in days. In his experience the morning after had been about promises you might keep and illusions you *wished* you could keep. Reality cast a harsh light, one that few romantic relationships could stand.

This time, however, reality added a lustre, a depth, that made him wonder if he'd understood anything at all about life before meeting Jeannie.

It was drizzling when they left the ship. "You hold Daisy," Hunter said. "I'll flag us down a cab." He was about to hand over the baby when he saw a familiar face in the crowd. "Damn it," he said. "That's my secretary."

"Hail the conquering hero!" Lisa called out, wav-

ing gaily through the crowd of debarking passengers.
"We got your faxes, Hunter. The top guns are singing
your praises!" She looked at Jeannie with open curiosity. "Hi," she said, extending her hand. "I'm
Lisa, Hunter's assistant."

"Jeannie Ross."

"Jeannie Ross," said Lisa, with a knowing look.
"You're the baby wrangler I spoke to on the phone.
What are you—" She glanced over at Hunter. "I
mean…" Her words trailed off.

"I took care of Daisy on the trip," said Jeannie.

Lisa's smile was knowing. She turned back to
Hunter. "You have to get to the office *pronto*. They
sent me over in a limo to bring you back in style."

Hunter muttered something under his breath. Jeannie smiled to herself. Knowing he had been sent on
the trip with the expectation of failure must make his
victory doubly sweet.

"Go," she said for his ears only. "I'll take a taxi
home."

"No way. You're taking the limo with us."

He was an amazing man. Another guy might have
played to his audience, making certain one and all
knew that they were lovers. Or treated her like an
employee.

Not Hunter. He didn't flaunt their relationship but
the fact that there was deep affection and respect was
obvious. The conclusions Lisa drew all depended
upon how perceptive she was—or how imaginative.

"I'm sorry she found us," he said as he walked

her to her door while the limo waited at the curb downstairs.

"So am I."

They lingered in the hallway, unwilling to let go of the magic.

"I'll call you," he said. "This isn't the end, Jeannie. It's only the beginning."

"OHMIGOD," said Kate the moment Jeannie opened the door. "I was right. You did it!"

"Shh!" She ushered Kate inside, then closed and locked the door behind her. "Must you broadcast everything to the entire building?"

Kate made an annoyed face. "I don't care about the building. I want details." She perched on the arm of the sofa and fixed Jeannie with a knowing look. "And the juicier the better."

"The pizza's getting cold," said Jeannie. "Let's eat."

"Uh-oh," said Kate, following Jeannie through the hallway. "This is serious."

Kate had the unnerving habit of being dead-on more often than not. This time was no exception. Jeannie had no idea how she was going to manage to dodge her questions for an entire evening.

"The crushed peppers are on the table," she said, opening the door to the fridge then grabbing a bottle of Diet Coke. "Do you want garlic salt?"

"I'd settle for a few answers."

Jeannie sat down opposite her friend and filled their

glasses with soda. "The cruise was great. I highly recommend it."

"And the bachelor father? How was he?"

She felt the heat moving upward from her chest. Thirty years old and she'd never once blushed—not until she met Hunter Phillips.

"So that's the way it is," said Kate. "I hope you were careful. These are dangerous times."

"I hope you'll take this the right way, Kate," she said, choosing her words with care, "but that's none of your business." She paused a moment. "Yes, we were careful."

Kate considered her for a long moment. Finally a smile lit her eyes. "I'm happy for you."

"Kate, don't—"

"I mean it, Jeannie. No jokes this time. Not even from an unemployed comic."

Jeannie arched a brow. "No lectures on the perfidy of men?"

"Not today." Kate regarded Jeannie with earnest intensity. "Just some advice."

Jeannie addressed herself to her pizza. She didn't want advice. She didn't want to let reality anywhere near the wonder she'd found with Hunter.

"Go slow," said Kate. "If it's the real thing, it'll still be there six months from now."

Jeannie laughed out loud. "What a strange thing to say! Do I look like a woman who's about to elope?"

"I know that look," said Kate, not laughing. "I looked that way when I ran off with the lawyer from

New Jersey.'' She paused. ''The one who broke my heart, I might add.''

''I think you're making too much out of this,'' Jeannie said. ''He might never call me again.'' Of course she didn't believe that, any more than she believed he would ever break her heart.

''He'll call. You made things wonderfully easy for him. No man can resist that.''

''You sound cynical, Kate.''

''Just realistic. You told me he was a shark when it came to business.''

The telephone rang. Jeannie's heart leaped into her throat.

''That's him,'' said Kate.

''I doubt it,'' said Jeannie. ''We just said goodbye a few hours ago.''

The phone rang a second time.

''If you don't answer it, I will,'' said Kate.

Jeannie stood up and reached for the wall phone.

''I miss you.'' Hunter's voice, deep and thrilling, curled itself inside her ear.

Kate, bless her heart, took her pizza into the living room. Jeannie sank back onto her chair.

''Me too,'' she said.

''Is your friend still there?''

''She's in the living room.''

''I want to come over.''

''What?''

''I want to see your face.''

''Hunter, I—''

''I'll be there in ten minutes.''

"But, Kate—"

"You can introduce us."

"The pizza—"

"Save me a slice."

"This is—"

"Ten minutes."

In a daze she made her way into the living room. "He's coming over."

Kate finished her slice of pizza. "I'm out of here."

"No," said Jeannie, "he wants to meet you."

"You're kidding. They *never* want to meet your friends."

"My hair!" Jeannie exclaimed. "My makeup! I'm a disaster."

"You look beautiful," Kate said, laughing. "You always do."

Jeannie, however, dashed to her bedroom to make repairs. In a million years she hadn't expected to hear from Hunter so soon, much less *see* him. She turned on the radio then tuned it to some soft music. Eyeliner. Shadow. A touch of lipstick.

"Don't you *dare* say anything to embarrass me, Kate," Jeannie called out as she walked through a cloud of Chanel No. 5, then headed toward the living room. "One word about whirlwind romances and, so help me, I'll—"

She stopped in the doorway to the living room. Hunter stood near the fireplace while Kate scurried around on the floor with a laughing Daisy in pursuit.

"Oh." Her breath left her body in a rush.

"Hi, Jeannie." Hunter met her eyes across the

room and her knees actually went weak. Up until that moment Jeannie had thought knees only went weak in nineteenth-century novels.

"Hello, Hunter." She wanted to run to him, feel his arms around her, catch the familiar, exciting scent of his skin.

Kate had been watching them. "I have an idea," she said, scrambling to her feet. "My sister's kids were here last week and they left half their toys on my living-room floor. Why don't I take Daisy and introduce her to her very own branch of F.A.O. Schwarz?"

Hunter looked at Jeannie.

"Kate lives across the hall," Jeannie said, heart pounding against her rib cage.

"Sure," said Hunter, looking at Kate. "If Daisy doesn't mind."

Kate scooped up Daisy into her arms. "What do you say?" she asked the baby.

Daisy grabbed a handful of Kate's hair and giggled.

"I think that's a yes," said Kate. "Knock on the door when you're...ready."

"Nice woman," said Hunter as the door closed behind Kate.

"Perceptive," said Jeannie.

"I—"

"You—"

No more words.

They came together in a rush of heat. His mouth was hungry against hers. She felt dizzy with longing.

Greedily, they touched and tasted until they f
onto the couch in a tangle of arms and legs.

"I missed you," Jeannie whispered against l
mouth.

"I couldn't stop thinking about you," he said, sl
ing his hands under her shirt. Waves of sensati
washed over her.

"We can't," she said. "Kate…the baby…" N
ther of them had expected spontaneous combustio

"Tomorrow," he said. "Dinner."

She nodded. She would have said yes to anythi
he suggested. "What about Daisy?"

"I'll find a sitter," he said, "if I have to c
Mother Teresa to do the job."

"Maybe Kate would," Jeannie said.

"We'll find a way," he said, kissing her hard.
promise you that."

TUESDAY NIGHT they went to a four-star French r
taurant while Kate watched Daisy. Candlelight fli
ered. Soft music played. They left their plates
touched while they held hands and looked into ea
other's eyes.

Wednesday night they kissed through an off-c
Broadway show.

Thursday night they took Daisy to Rumpelmayer
then the three of them enjoyed a carriage ride throu
the Park.

Saying good-night was torture. The hours th
spent apart stretched out like years. Their old lives
longer fit. Those four nights on the ship had bond

them as a family in a way neither could have expected.

Jeannie wandered around her apartment, listening to old records and daydreaming. *This isn't enough,* she thought. She wanted to fall asleep in Hunter's arms and wake up to the sound of Daisy's laughter. She'd had a taste of how wonderful life could be and she was determined to grab happiness with both hands.

Hunter, riding on his success with the *Star of the Atlantic,* kept his office door closed during the day so he could stare out the window and think about Jeannie. That incredible burst of turbo-charged energy and creativity he'd experienced aboard ship was just out of reach and he knew that Jeannie was the key to bringing it back again.

"So now what, Daisy?" he asked as he tossed a foam rubber basketball through the hoop attached to the far wall of his office. "Do we or don't we?"

"Daah," said Daisy from her playpen next to his desk.

"Is that yes or no?"

She looked at him, cornflower-blue eyes wide, and popped her thumb into her mouth.

"Not talking, huh?" He rolled the basketball toward her, laughing as her little feet pumped the air as if she wanted to kick it. "I'm looking for answers and all you can do is give me the silent treatment."

Truth was, these days even Daisy wasn't herself when Jeannie wasn't around. As for Hunter, he couldn't sleep, couldn't work, could think of only one way to bring all the disparate parts of his life together.

At first he denied it. Then he considered it.

And by Friday morning Hunter knew exactly what he was going to do.

"THIS IS A STRANGE PLACE for lunch," said Jeannie as she settled into her seat opposite Hunter and Daisy. "Most people don't grab a sandwich in a hospital cafeteria unless they have to." Apprehension swooped down on her. "Hunter! Is something wrong?"

"Nothing's wrong," he said, looking terribly serious.

"Thank God," she breathed, slumping back in her seat. "Then why are we here?"

He leaned forward. Even Daisy looked serious. "It's not working, Jeannie. Dinner...dancing...it's just not cutting it."

She looked down at the scarred surface of the table. "I'm sorry you feel that way."

"Don't you?"

She met his eyes and saw herself, and all she was, reflected in them. "What—what exactly are you talking about, Hunter?"

"Let's get married."

The words hit her with the force of a physical blow. "Married?"

He laughed, leaning across the Formica table and gathering her hands in his. "Hitched. Wed. Whatever you want to call it. Let's just go and do it. A friend of mine's a doctor here. We could have the blood tests done right now then go see about a license.''

"But we—I mean..." *Come on, Jeannie, you can do better than that.* She knew the idea was crazy but, for the life of her, she couldn't imagine why.

"I'm not eating or sleeping or working worth a damn. When I'm not with you, I'm thinking about you...about how much I want to see you. When I *am* with you, I'm worried about how little time we have. It can't go on like this, Jeannie."

Jeannie swallowed hard. "When we said goodbye this morning, I found I missed you and Daisy so much I thought my heart was going to break." Before meeting Hunter and Daisy, she'd accepted loneliness as her punishment. Now she felt as if she had been standing alone in a dark, forbidding room and somebody turned on the lights, showing her that the monsters in the darkness were only her own dreams finally taking form.

"It's crazy," she said.

"I don't deny that. But it's the real thing, isn't it, Jeannie? The whole damn package right here in front of us."

"It's perfect," she breathed. "All of it. The way it is with us...with Daisy. It's so perfect that it scares me." She paused. Happy endings were possible. She had to believe that.

"I'm not married," he said. "You're not married—"

"But I—"

"No 'buts,'" he broke in. "There's nothing stopping us."

"Hunter, I—"

"So what's it going to be?" he demanded. "Are you willing to take a chance?"

She thought of her empty apartment, of her cold and lonely bed, of the endless days and nights stretching out ahead of her into infinity.

"Yes," she said, starting to laugh. "I'm willing to take a chance!"

THEY HURRIED up to the third floor where Hunter's friend performed the blood tests while lecturing on the wonders of marriage.

"Audrey's a newlywed," Hunter said.

"Five weeks, three days, and six hours," said Audrey, flashing her wedding band. "I highly recommend it."

They took that as an omen.

Of course, they took everything as an omen that afternoon. The light turned green the moment they reached the corner and Hunter said it meant the gods wanted them to get married. Jeannie saw a pot of shamrocks in the window of a shop that sold Waterford crystal and she said the luck of the Irish was on their side.

And when the first cab Hunter whistled for screeched to a halt and welcomed them, they knew they were home free.

They stopped at their respective apartments for birth certificates and ID, then cabbed downtown to a city office building where they filled out an application for a marriage license. Even Daisy seemed filled with excitement.

"You're thirty-four?" Jeannie asked, peering down at the information on his side of the form.

"I look older?"

"Younger."

He glanced down at her side. "An April Fool's Day baby?"

She glared at him. "One bad joke, Hunter, and so help me..."

There was so much to learn, so many wonderful things to share, and so little time to get ready.

HUNTER FOUND HIMSELF thinking more and more about family as their wedding day rapidly drew near.

He had no illusions about how his own parents would react to his upcoming marriage. His anger over their treatment of Callie's pregnancy still burned, but these days that anger was laced with regret.

"Callie would've been crazy about you," he said to Jeannie one night over dinner.

"I wish I'd met her. I keep trying to imagine you as a little boy. It would be nice to speak to an eyewitness." She paused. "I don't suppose you'd consider asking your parents to fly in for the wedding."

"You're right," he said. "I wouldn't."

His family wouldn't come if asked.

Her family would come, but they weren't invited.

He looked over at Jeannie. Her smile was as open and sunny as Daisy's toothless grin. There was no reason for the persistent sense that things weren't exactly as they seemed. Why look for trouble, he thought. They'd have a lifetime to work out their family problems.

But they only had a few days to plan a wedding.

THE SALESWOMAN at the boutique favored Jeannie and Kate with a wide professional smile. "Good afternoon, ladies," she said. "And how can I help you?"

"I'm looking for something simple and elegant," Jeannie said. "Preferably in off-white."

"For a special occasion?"

She looked at Kate then back to the saleswoman. "You could say that."

"She's getting married," Kate volunteered, shaking her head in amazement. "Tomorrow."

"Oh, how wonderful!" The saleswoman's smile got a little bit wider. "I think we can—" She stopped, peering more closely at the two women before her. "Haven't I seen you ladies before?"

Jeannie started to laugh. "Last week," she said. "The black spaghetti-strap dance dress."

"Ah, yes," said the saleswoman. "You were going on a cruise, if I remember correctly."

"It was a whirlwind romance," Kate said. "One whiff of salt air and that's all she wrote."

"Evidently salt air is more effective than French perfume," said the saleswoman. "You met the gentleman on shipboard?"

"Well, not exactly," Jeannie said, wishing she

could disappear into the dressing room and come out when the wedding was over. "We'd met a few days before." *Oh God,* she thought, as Kate burst into gales of laughter. *It sounds as though I picked him up in a bar and ran off with him.*

Kate was still laughing as she followed Jeannie into the dressing room.

"Enjoy yourself, Ms. Big Mouth," Jeannie muttered as she slipped out of her trousers and shirt. "You were more than willing to volunteer information about everything else. Why didn't you tell her I worked for Hunter and make me sound respectable?"

Kate made a face as she sat down on the boudoir chair in the corner of the room. "You got yourself into this mess, Ross. I'm just enjoying the show."

Jeannie tried on two beige dresses and an eggshell-white gown in quick succession. "Too fancy," she said, "too glitzy, too boring."

Kate and the saleswoman exchanged looks.

"What exactly are you looking for?" the saleswoman asked. "Maybe something in a gentle yellow?"

"How about a suit?" Kate volunteered. "Something classic."

"In silk," Jeannie said. She turned to Kate. "I could wear a camisole under it and my grandmother's pearls."

The saleswoman brightened. "I have just the ticket." Moments later she was back, bearing the most perfect suit in a cream-colored silk that begged to be worn against bare skin.

"That's it," said Kate, her eyes suspiciously wet.

"You look beautiful," said the saleswoman, smelling victory.

Jeannie turned slowly to face the mirror. "Ohmigod," she said, staring at her reflection. "I'm getting married tomorrow!"

"THIS IS VERY IMPORTANT," Hunter told the salesclerk at You Must Have Been A Beautiful Baby, a boutique off Madison Avenue. "We need the fanciest dress you have in the place."

"Special occasion?" asked the woman, chucking Daisy under the chin.

"A wedding," said Hunter, liking the sound.

"Well, well," said the woman with a knowing smile. "I think I have just the thing."

Any other time Hunter would have felt like Gulliver in the Land of the Lilliputs, but for some reason he thoroughly enjoyed the process of picking out the perfect outfit for Daisy to wear to the wedding.

In fact, by the time they'd settled on a frilly dress the same color as Daisy's eyes, Hunter found himself really getting into the spirit of things.

"Over there," he said, pointing toward a display case to the left of the register. "Those lacy socks."

"Ahh," said the salesclerk, her eyes dancing with delight. "And a wonderful choice they are, sir. The lace trim was handworked by nuns in a Swiss convent."

"Daah?" Daisy tugged at his ear, as if she couldn't believe her ears.

"Whatever the lady says," he mumbled, knowing ad-speak when he heard it.

"Would you like a pair for your daughter?"

"She's not my daughter," he said quickly, "and yes, I'd like a pair."

"Not your daughter?" The woman's perfectly made-up face creased in a frown. "I thought she said da-da."

"She doesn't talk yet," Hunter said, wondering why the fascination with Daisy's parentage. "Now, about the socks..."

Ten minutes later Hunter, Daisy, and a big fat shopping bag filled with obscenely expensive baby clothes escaped the clutches of the eager saleswoman. He could still hear the sound of the cash register ringing up the string of purchases.

"Don't think I'm setting a precedent," he said to Daisy as they headed for home. "This is a once-in-a-lifetime thing."

The next time he spent money like that on clothing, it had better be for a new Armani jacket to replace the one he'd lost to Daisy's apple juice.

"HOW DO I LOOK?" asked Jeannie for the hundredth time as the rented car neared the little town outside the city limits where the wedding would take place.

"Beautiful," said Kate. "Radiant." She narrowed her eyes purposefully. "Much too good for a crazy woman."

"It *is* crazy, isn't it?" Jeannie said, smiling broadly. "Sane people don't do things like this."

"That's true," said Kate, "but sane people miss a lot of fun."

Jeannie stared at her friend. "Is that encouragement I hear from you?"

"Don't let it go to your head," Kate said. "I do think you're crazy, but at least I understand."

"You like Hunter?"

"It's not Hunter that worries me right now, honey. It's you."

"Me?" Jeannie's voice rose in surprise. "I'd never do anything to hurt him."

"Maybe not," said Kate, "but I just can't shake the feeling that there's something you're not quite telling him."

"That's ridiculous."

"Probably is," said Kate agreeably. "But ever since we met I've been convinced you're a lot more complicated than you seem."

"Isn't everyone?" Jeannie asked. "I'll bet you have a few stories in your background."

Kate feigned surprise. "*Moi?* My life's an open book."

The driver whirred down the glass partition. "We're here, ladies." The car came to a stop in front of the judge's office.

Jeannie peered out the window. Hunter and Daisy waited on the sidewalk. Hunter wore a navy suit, cream-colored shirt, and striped tie. Her heart bumped up against her breastbone as she noticed his shaggy hair had been newly trimmed in honor of the occasion. Daisy was decked out in a pale blue dress with matching socks with ruffled cuffs. His best man was standing on the steps, scanning the street for the rest of the wedding party.

"Will you look at him," Kate said, whistling low. "Is that a gorgeous man or not?"

"That is definitely a gorgeous man," said Jeannie. "What's his name?"

Jeannie laughed. "I guess we're not talking about Hunter, are we? That's Trey Whittaker, a photographer friend of Hunter's." Obviously Kate's antimale stance was weakening.

Trey said something to Hunter. Hunter looked toward the street as Jeannie stepped from the car.

The look on his face when his eyes met hers erased the last of her fears.

This is right, her heart said as he reached for her hand. Crazy. Impractical. Illogical.

But right.

"You're beautiful, Jeannie."

"So are you," she whispered.

Daisy reached out to tug at Jeannie's earring and, laughing, Jeannie ducked out of the baby's reach.

"Come on, Daisy," Hunter said as they walked up the steps to the judge's office. "You're still on your good behavior. Jeannie and I aren't married yet. She might still change her mind."

Not a chance, thought Jeannie.

Maybe it was crazy, leaping into marriage with someone she barely knew, but somehow it felt like the sanest thing she'd done in years.

JEANNIE STAYED amazingly calm during the ceremony. Her voice sounded clear and confident. Hunter stumbled once during the vows when Daisy, in Kate's arms, leaned over and tugged hard on his hair, but he recovered quickly.

The words to the wedding vows held a resonance he hadn't expected. Like everybody else, he'd heard them a thousand times over, in movies, on television, at the weddings of friends.

Quaint, a little flowery, as familiar as his phone number or street address.

But when a woman with a heart as beautiful as her face was saying those words to you and when you were saying those same words right back to her and meaning them—well, it made a man think.

"I do," said Jeannie, her voice strong.

"I do," said Hunter, amazed.

Kate and Trey burst into cheers as he took Jeannie in his arms.

Tears glistened in her blue eyes and he suspected his own eyes were a little moist. He couldn't remember a time when he felt more connected with his life, more certain that he'd made the right choice, found the right woman at the right time.

He was on his way.

FEW PLACES in Manhattan were more beautiful than Tavern on the Green.

Set at the edge of Central Park not far from Lincoln Center, it was a jewel of a restaurant. No matter the season, the trees inside and out were strung with twinkling diamond lights that added to the air of genteel glamour.

Hunter and Jeannie had planned to take her maid of honor and best man to Tavern on the Green for an intimate dinner. Kate and Trey, however, had taken matters into their own hands, arranging a combination bridal shower/wedding reception for the newlyweds.

A crowd of people from C V & S showed up, along with photographers, stylists, and bookers Jeannie had worked with. If it seemed odd to anyone that neither Hunter's nor Jeannie's family was present, no one said a word. They were too busy eating, drinking, and teasing the bride and groom.

"Hunter knows a good deal when he sees one," said an ad exec with a full head of red curls and impressive cleavage as she sized up Jeannie from head to toe. "I'll bet he never gave you a chance to say no."

"Good going, Phillips," said a bean counter from the financial department. "She's not only gorgeous, she works with kids for a living. Who needs day care when you have Jeannie."

"A built-in baby expert," said Walter Grantham, by way of congratulations. "Brilliant strategy, Hunter. Exactly what I'd expect of our top ad exec. I told you that you needed a wife to take care of things at home. Once the honeymoon is over, I want you back to work in top form."

Grantham drifted away toward the open bar.

Hunter drew Jeannie toward a secluded corner behind a ficus tree strung with white lights.

"Grantham's a jerk," he said bluntly. "They're all jerks. I hope you don't think I—"

"Of course I don't," she broke in, raising on tiptoe so she could kiss him. "There are easier ways to find a baby-sitter than marrying one."

He glanced back at the laughing throng, most of whom were speculating on which of them had snagged the better deal.

"Let's go," said Hunter. "No one's watching. We can make our getaway."

"Go where?"

"Anywhere."

"We can't do that, Hunter. Our friends—they'd wonder where we went."

"We have to. We're the wedding couple. It's expected of us."

"How do we sneak Daisy out?"

He flashed her a mock leer. "We don't."

"Hunter!"

"Keep it down. Don't draw attention to us."

"You can't leave Daisy here."

"Kate's keeping her overnight."

She started to laugh. "You're a wicked man."

"Absolutely."

"Your place or mine?"

"Neither," he said, heading for the door.

"Hunter, I—"

"Trust me," he said as they slipped outside. "You won't be sorry."

Chapter Seven

Jeannie sat on the edge of the marble bathtub in the Plaza Hotel and took another in a series of deep calming breaths. The classic wedding night jitters. Who would ever have expected it?

"This is ridiculous," she murmured, pressing a cool cloth to the back of her neck. She and Hunter had already shared the pleasures to be found in a common bed. They'd entered this marriage with their eyes wide open, with enthusiasm and the certainty that they could make it work.

Unfortunately she hadn't entered into it with a clear conscience.

Kate had been right when she said that Jeannie was withholding something. She didn't know how her friend had sensed it, but Kate's words had hit Jeannie like a blow. The truth had that strange ability.

She should have told him. It would have been so easy that very first night over pastrami sandwiches when there had been nothing between them except professional interest. He would have understood. Any man who would take in his sister's infant and raise her as his own would understand. The terror. The guilt. The long road back. He would have understood it all.

But she'd let that opportunity pass. She'd never been one for baring her soul in public. Not even when the pain was new and fresh had she been able to talk about it to anyone. Like a wounded animal, she had retreated into her own cave and nursed her broken spirit until she could once again come out and face the world.

Her pencil had hesitated on the marriage license application, stumbling over the question about marital status. *Single. Divorced. Widowed.* All she had to do was check the proper box and take her chances.

But that would mean dredging up old wounds. Puncturing the fantasy balloon of happiness that she and Hunter had created.

"I did the right thing," she said to her reflection in the mirror. They belonged together, Hunter and Daisy and herself. They were a family. From the first moment she'd seen him with his little girl she'd known it, almost as if it had been preordained. She deserved this happiness. Telling him about those who had come before wouldn't change anything. Nothing would bring them back. Nothing would ever destroy the love she had for them.

And nothing could make her love Hunter and Daisy any more than she already did.

She was committed to them. To the idea of family. To the future that was once again hers for the asking.

HUNTER HAD NEVER given much thought to the concept of a wedding night. Back in the days when bride and groom came together in innocence after the nuptials he supposed the wedding night was a time of great anticipation and anxiety, fraught with all sorts of emotions he'd figured himself too sophisticated to fall prey to.

He was wrong.

Marriage made it all different.

He didn't understand how or why, but the simple act of repeating those vows with a full heart had changed everything. He wanted Jeannie with the same driving passion he'd felt for her before the ceremony. Only now there was a sense of continuity at play, the deeper knowledge that each action, each promise made between them, had a resonance that affected every other part of his life.

Now if his wife would only come out of the bathroom maybe he could tell her all that was in his heart.

JEANNIE opened the bathroom door slowly. The bedroom was dark, lit only by two flickering candles on the dressing table near the window. Someone had turned down the covers and a fresh pale pink rosebud rested on each of the pillows. She smiled to herself as she headed toward the hallway. Knowing Hunter he'd probably eaten the requisite chocolate mint.

He was waiting for her in the drawing room. She paused in the doorway. He stood by the window, his shirtless torso illuminated by the lights of the city below.

Champagne chilled in a silver bucket. A tray of fresh shrimp, perfectly arranged, waited next to the champagne. All she really saw was her husband.

"Hunter."

He turned. The sight of her in her satin teddy knocked the breath from his body. She was so small, so perfectly made—and she was his.

Ah, yes. *His.*

Words came easily as a rule. He knew the words that would sell a car or convince a woman she needed a new perfume. But when it came to words that would express how he felt, he was as tongue-tied as the next guy. Maybe more. He had no experience with emotion. His family never talked about how they felt. He'd grown up without a vocabulary of dreams.

As his wife glided toward him he would have sold his soul for the words to tell her how deeply he cared.

THEIR FIRST NIGHT together had been a comedy of errors.

Their wedding night was a fantasy come true.

She was soft where he was not. He demanded all and she yielded that and more. Boundaries melted. Barriers disappeared.

She lay there on the welcoming bed while he watched the play of light and shadow across her satiny skin. The movement of her hand against him was a miracle.

"You've changed my life," she whispered, her breath as soft as angel wings.

He stroked her hair back from her cheek. "You've done the same for me."

"I never dreamed anything like this could possibly happen."

He leaned up on one elbow. "What did you dream about, Jeannie?" There were so many things he didn't know about her.

She ducked her head, pressing her face against his chest. "Happiness."

"Have you found it?"

"What do you think?"

He rolled her onto her back and poised himself above her. "I think we both have."

Arching her hips, she grasped him by the buttocks and drew him down to her. "Show me," she said, her voice low and seductive. "Make me believe it, Hunter." Again and again until there was nothing she could do but believe.

Her words turned him to flame. He grabbed her hands and held them over her head, pinning them against the pillow. She moaned low in her throat, urging him on.

She gave herself up to his will. She loved knowing he was stronger, that what they shared was so powerful that she was helpless before it. Surrender was all the sweeter knowing he understood the deeper meaning of all she gave to him.

He found her center yet again, growing stronger with each cry of pleasure he drew from her. She wrapped her legs around his waist, arching higher and higher, drawing him more deeply inside her body.

Making him long for her soul.

DAWN WAS GILDING the trees in the park outside their window when they finally fell asleep. Jeannie curled in toward Hunter as if she couldn't get enough of the feel and smell of his skin. Hunter enveloped her in his arms, drunk on the perfume of her body, the soft sound of her heartbeat.

Jeannie awoke a little before eleven in the morning. There was no surprise. No disorientation. Waking up in Hunter's arms seemed as right and natural as breathing. His dark hair brushed his forehead and she smoothed it back with a gentle hand. He looked younger in sleep, as if she were glimpsing the boy he once was. His strong jaw seemed less stubborn; the sensual line of his mouth begged for the touch of her lips.

There was something terribly intimate in watching a man sleep, even if that man was her husband. Men prided themselves on control both real and imagined. Asleep a man was as vulnerable as a child. She had a quick memory of another wedding, of youthful dreams, but she pushed them away.

This was a different time and place—and she was a vastly different woman from the wide-eyed girl she'd once been.

The dreams, however, were still the same.

Out of nowhere had come this second chance—an opportunity to recover the happiness she'd thought gone forever.

Hunter had a handful of days off—a special gift

from Grantham and the other bigwigs at C V & S—
and they'd planned to enjoy the Plaza Hotel and the
environs. But Jeannie had other ideas.

"Hunter." She nudged his shoulder.

"Mmmph?" He opened one sleepy hazel-green
eye then grinned. "So I didn't dream last night."

"You didn't dream last night."

He reached for her left hand and brought it to his
lips. The gold wedding band was warm from her skin.
"Jeannie Phillips," he said. "I like the sound."

"So do I."

He glanced toward the small clock on the nightstand. "We slept through breakfast."

"So we did."

He pulled her down across his body and gave her
a playful swat on the rump. "You don't sound repentant."

"I'm not."

"Here we are in one of the best suites in the Plaza
Hotel and we're sleeping away the time."

"We didn't just sleep, Hunter," she pointed out.

"Order us some breakfast," he said, tossing off the
covers. "I'll grab a shower and after we eat we can
play tourists."

Jeannie touched his arm. "That's what I wanted to
talk to you about."

"There's someplace you want to go?"

"Absolutely."

"Name it, Mrs. Phillips. Your wish is my command."

"Home," she said.

"You're kidding."

"No, I'm not. I can't think of anything I'd rather do than pick up Daisy and go home."

"Now there's something we need to talk about." He looked at her. "Where's home going to be?"

Jeannie stared at him. "I haven't thought about it."

"Me neither, but it seems like it's time."

"There's always my place," she ventured. "It's comfortable and roomy." She hesitated. "The only thing is, my landlord will be back in February so my place is a temporary thing."

"Then there isn't much of a choice, is there? We'll live in my place."

"But I've never even seen your place." She could just imagine Hunter's apartment: the typical bachelor lair with a baby crib and playpen added for good measure. "Black furniture, gray rugs, and a lot of chrome?"

"Bingo," said Hunter.

Jeannie sighed and fell back against the pillows.

Laughing, he leaned over her. "Two bedrooms," he said.

Jeannie perked up the slightest bit.

"Eat-in kitchen."

"I'm beginning to like the sound of it."

"And we can redecorate."

She threw her arms around his neck. "Come on," she said, leaping from the bed. "Let's get Daisy and go shopping."

HUNTER HAD NEVER MET a woman quite like the one he'd taken as a wife.

"Bloomingdale's?" she said, wrinkling her nose in

distaste. "Too trendy."

Macy's was too slow to deliver. Specialty stores were too expensive.

"So where are we going to shop?" he asked as they walked to Kate's place to fetch their daughter. "New Jersey?"

"That's right," said Jeannie.

Hunter groaned. "Somehow I never expected to spend our honeymoon in New Jersey."

"I hung on to my car when I moved here last year. We'll be at the store before you know it."

"Are you one of those women who were born to shop?"

She laughed and linked her arm through his. "Only when there's a reason to shop."

"Because it's Friday?"

"No," she said, poking him in the side. "Because we need to set up housekeeping as a family."

He had a child to raise.

And now he had a wife.

But a family?

THE FURNITURE salesman hovered around like a hawk over its unsuspecting prey. Hunter and Jeannie and Daisy had logged more miles in that New Jersey warehouse than a trio of Olympic hopefuls.

"I don't know," Jeannie said, considering a huge leather chair with interest. "I think you should ask my husband."

Hunter had to grin at those words. Two days ago

he'd been a single man. Today he was part of a family.

Imagine that.

"Sir?" The salesman turned toward him. "Perhaps you should give the chair a try."

"Looks great," he said. His butt had been in so many chairs and sofas that afternoon that he was sure he'd need a rubber donut before the day was through.

"Bob is right," Jeannie said, switching Daisy to her left shoulder. "This will be your chair. You really should sit in it."

He did. "This is great," he said, putting his feet up on the matching ottoman. "I feel like Robert Young in *Father Knows Best.*"

Jeannie gave him a skeptical look.

"I'm not kidding," he said. "All I need is a beagle to bring me my slippers."

"You've been in advertising too long," Jeannie said, laughing out loud. "You sound like a commercial."

Bob, the salesman, looked bewildered.

"We'll take it," said Hunter. "And that big sofa over there." And the armoire. Nightstands. Dressing table. Solid oak kitchen set with a matching high chair for Daisy.

"We spent a fortune in there," Jeannie said as he drove her car back to Manhattan.

"Cheaper than Bloomingdale's," he said blithely, casting her a quick look. "Isn't that what you said?"

"I didn't say we should buy the entire store, Hunter! We went crazy in there."

"So what. You only get married once, right?"

A sharp stab of guilt pierced Jeannie's heart. She busied herself with rummaging through her pocketbook for Daisy's ring of plastic keys.

"We have a lot of things to talk about," he continued as they exited the George Washington Bridge.

She swallowed hard. "Such as?"

"Money, for one. I make a lot." He quoted her a number. "If the Christmas bonus is up to par, it could be even more."

She was silent for a moment. "My income isn't quite as impressive, but it's not bad." She quoted him a number.

"How do you feel about joint checking and savings?"

"Fine," she said. She'd always believed in the fifty-fifty concept of marriage. "How do you feel about scrubbing bathrooms?"

"We've invented self-cleaning ovens. Why not self-cleaning toilets."

"But until then?"

"Fifty-fifty," he said. "In everything."

She looked at her husband and a big grin spread across her face. "I may have been impulsive," she said, "but I certainly was smart."

AS FAR AS HUNTER was concerned, the best part of living in New York was getting out of it.

"I can't believe you haven't driven out to Long Island," he said to Jeannie as he drove across the city line into Nassau County on the last day of their honeymoon. "Everyone checks out the Hamptons at least once."

"Not me," said his wife. "I have a built-in aversion to trendiness."

"Jones Beach isn't trendy," he said, thinking about the enormous stretch of beaches most New Yorkers loved. "You won't see a bottle of Evian water for miles."

"Good," said Jeannie. "Water should come from the tap, not the gourmet section of the grocery store."

"You're opinionated," Hunter said. "I like that in a woman."

"Of course you do," said Jeannie. "That and breasts the size of honeydew melons."

"Are you ever going to forget Marcy?" he asked, shaking his head in bemusement.

"A woman never forgets the moment she met her husband. If Daisy hadn't wet her diaper, we wouldn't be sitting here now. You'd probably be off in the Hamptons with Marcy or some other blond bombshell and I'd—"

"No." He turned away from the road for an instant and met her eyes. "I would have found you, Jeannie. Don't ever doubt that."

"It's a big world," she said lightly, obviously pleased. "Happiness can be easy to miss. Sometimes you have to almost lose it before you know it's even there."

Maybe on another day, in a different mood, he might have followed up on that statement, but not today.

"This is the life," he said, veering sharply away from tricky emotional territory. "Clear skies, bright sunshine, a full tank of gas—it doesn't get much better than this."

She hit him over the head with the folded road map that had rested on her lap. "You're quite the romantic," she said dryly. "If you start singing the praises of a five-speed transmission, I'll get off at the next corner."

He eyeballed the odometer. "You've put over one hundred thousand miles on this baby in less than five years. Where'd you take it?"

"I told you I've worked just about everywhere in this country."

"What about since you've been in New York?"

"The Catskills. The Adirondacks," she said. "Over to the Berkshires." She grinned. "The Poconos."

He started to laugh. "The Poconos? Heart-shaped tubs and waterbeds?"

"There's more to the Poconos than honeymoon havens," she said primly. "There's fresh air and lakes and open space. It's a wonderful place to raise a family."

He caught a glimpse of Daisy in the back seat. Today she wore a sailor's outfit complete with hat and it seemed to him that she was growing bigger before his eyes. Where they lived wasn't important to Daisy now, but the time would come when he would have to give serious thought to things like schools and play groups and all the other things that went hand in hand with raising kids in the 90s.

Sometimes it seemed as if every part of his life— from where he lived right now to how he dressed— had been affected by Daisy's arrival.

If someone had told him this time last year that he'd be married and raising a kid before the next twelve months were over, he would have laughed in his face.

If they'd told him he'd spend a lazy Sunday afternoon at Jones Beach with a plastic pail and shovel, he would have suggested therapy.

And if they'd told him he'd actually be having a good time—well, truth really was stranger than fiction.

JONES BEACH State Park was a huge, sprawling selection of individual beaches that curved along the south shore of Long Island. There were fishing beaches, Zach's Bay with its amphitheater, and an old-fashioned expanse of boardwalk second to none.

Finding a parking spot was problematic and he breathed a sigh of relief when he finally angled into a spot near the back of one of the numbered lots.

"Looks like everyone in New York had the same idea," he said as they took their gear from the trunk.

"It's a gorgeous spring day," Jeannie said, slipping on her dark glasses and reaching for the cooler. "Who wouldn't want to enjoy the outdoors?"

"I don't think George Washington had so many supplies at Valley Forge." Hunter shifted Daisy to his other shoulder as he yanked out the beach umbrella and the rest of the paraphernalia. "Did we really need all this junk?"

"Of course we did," said Jeannie. "The amount of equipment is in inverse proportion to the size of the child. It's a law of nature."

"If that's the case, we'll need an eighteen-wheeler before Daisy's tenth birthday."

"Grump," she said as they made their way through the parking lot. "Just wait until you see Daisy's face when she sees the beach."

"Do you think she'll like it?"

"She'll love it."

"How do you know?"

"She likes bath time, doesn't she?"

Hunter shot Jeannie a look of pure disbelief. "A bathtub is one thing," he said. "The Atlantic Ocean is something else." Suddenly Daisy seemed a lot smaller to him than she had a few minutes earlier. "I'm acting like a jerk, aren't I? The beach is no big deal."

She raised up on tiptoe and kissed his cheek. "You're acting like you care. I think that makes you pretty terrific."

He liked the gesture even if he wasn't entirely comfortable with her observation.

And she noticed.

"You amaze me, Hunter," she said. "C V & S's rising star can't take a compliment."

"Words are cheap," he said, a grin curving his mouth. "Actions are better."

"Patience," she said. He could almost see her eyes twinkling through her dark glasses. "The day is young."

"YOU WERE RIGHT," said Hunter an hour later. "She loves it."

"I told you so," said Jeannie. "Daisy is very adaptable."

He looked at the little girl sitting between his knees on the wet sand. "This kid has more guts than any two men I know."

"And why not," Jeannie said. "She's a Phillips, isn't she?"

"I thought she was going to break away from me and swim across the Atlantic," he said, laughing. "It was like seeing my sister all over again."

Once again Jeannie seemed to understand his mood before he did. "Get up, lazybones," she said, scrambling to her feet. "Let's jump the waves."

"With Daisy?"

"Tiny waves," Jeannie said. "We'll only go in up to our ankles."

He and Jeannie each held one of Daisy's hands and the baby squealed with delight each time they lifted her into the air as the waves foamed around their ankles and calves.

"Oh, will you look at that adorable little girl!" A woman, hugely pregnant, stopped in her tracks. "How old is she?"

"Almost nine months," said Jeannie.

The woman leaned into Daisy and touched her

cheek. "You beautiful little thing. You look just like your mommy and daddy."

"We appreciate the compliment," said Jeannie, who knew the drill, "but she's not—"

"Thanks," said Hunter, with a nod of his head. "We think she's pretty terrific, too."

THEY CALLED OUT for pizza that night. Pepperoni for Hunter. Mushroom for Jeannie. Daisy had a jar of lamb and vegetables. Hunter looked at her dinner with dismay.

"Hurry up with those teeth, Daise," he said as Jeannie put the spoon to the baby's mouth. "You're going to love pizza."

"She will if she's her daddy's girl," Jeannie said.

There it was again. He started to say what he always said, that he loved Daisy with all his heart but that he wasn't her father and it was better for everyone to keep that one very important fact in mind. But for the second time that day, the words didn't come.

Everyone had told him that parenthood was more than a question of biology, that it was the small things—the feedings and the dirty diapers and the worrying—that made you a parent.

For months he'd felt as if he were rushing headlong toward disaster. His social life had been shot to hell. His career was headed for the dumper.

And when it came to Daisy, he'd stumbled along through the dark, praying the mistakes he made wouldn't haunt Daisy twenty years later.

How many times in the past eight months had he

sat here at this kitchen table, eating pizza while he fed Daisy? The routine was as familiar to him as his telephone number.

But tonight everything seemed different.

Jeannie's laughter seemed to fill the empty places in the room—and maybe one or two of the empty places inside his heart.

He pushed back his chair and stood up. "Come on, kiddo," he said gruffly, lifting Daisy from her high chair. "Bath time."

"Hunter." Jeannie's voice was soft, slightly puzzled. "Aren't you forgetting something?"

He stood in the doorway, frowning. "Water, soap, baby—"

"Me."

"I have other plans for you."

She stood up and walked over to him and Daisy. "It's a package deal, Hunter," she said, hugging them both. "First Daisy's bath and then..." She wiggled her eyebrows mischievously.

"A shower," he said, meeting her eyes. "A long, hot shower."

"And then—?"

He kissed her hard. "A longer and hotter night."

Chapter Eight

"So what are you and Daisy going to do today?" Hunter asked as he knotted his tie in front of the hall mirror.

Jeannie reached up to smooth his shirt collar. It was Monday morning and real life was upon them once again. "After Daisy wakes up, I think we'll walk over to my apartment and pack up my things."

He gestured toward the desk. "I have the number of a moving company in there someplace. You might want to give them a call."

"Don't need one," she said as he turned away from the mirror and drew her into his arms. "I could fit most of my things in two shopping bags."

He pulled back and looked at her. "Two shopping bags?"

"Maybe three. I travel light."

He chuckled then tilted her face up for a kiss. "I hate to leave."

She kissed him back. "I'm going to miss you."

"If you kiss me again like that I might stay home."

"Great," she said, laughing. "Then you can wait for the furniture delivery men this afternoon."

She was still laughing as the door closed behind him.

Daisy woke up, a little cranky from the budding tooth. Once the baby was cleaned and dressed, Jeannie popped her into the old high chair.

Sunshine streamed through the casement windows—a miracle in New York City. She tuned the radio to an oldies station that had her singing along in seconds. Daisy gobbled up every last bit of her cereal then burped obligingly.

Just a few weeks ago, the thought of her Hawaiian assignment had her eagerly marking the days on her calendar. Now she couldn't imagine anything more wonderful—or satisfying—than living the life of wife and mother.

She supposed it was out of fashion to admit to such feelings, but she'd always found enormous satisfaction in caring for her family. Her talents were domestic, as were her greatest joys, and she considered herself lucky beyond measure to have a brand-new family to love.

"Look at you," said Kate twenty minutes later as she followed Jeannie and the baby into Jeannie's old apartment. "You look so happy it's disgusting."

"I *am* happy," Jeannie said, lifting Daisy from the stroller and placing her on the rug. "Can you believe it?"

Kate perched on the arm of the sofa. "After the

past week, I can believe just about anything. Talk about whirlwind romances...."

"Which brings me to the sixty-four-thousand-dollar question," said Jeannie. "What's with you and Trey Whittaker?"

Kate turned an incriminating shade of scarlet. "I don't know," she mumbled.

"Kate!"

"Really," said Kate, sliding down onto the sofa. "I'm not sure if there's anything between us."

"He's adorable."

"I've noticed."

"And you look adorable together."

Kate tossed a sofa pillow at Jeannie who tossed it right back at her.

"Just because you two happy romantics were struck by the thunderbolt, don't think the rest of us have been."

"Miracles happen," said Jeannie, redirecting Daisy's attention away from teething on the leg of the sofa.

Kate sat up straight and scrutinized her. "There you go again. There are times when I'd swear you had a secret life going for you somewhere."

"You've been reading too many mysteries, Kate."

"Maybe," Kate said, not sounding at all convinced. "But I have the persistent feeling there's more to you than meets the eye."

"You've missed your calling," Jeannie said dryly. "Forget comedy. You could give Agatha Christie a run for her money."

"So tell me," said Kate. "What did your families have to say about the big news?"

Jeannie began sorting through the magazines on the coffee table. "We haven't told them yet."

"You haven't told them?" Kate leaped to her feet, startling Daisy into dropping her key ring.

"For heaven sake, Kate, you don't have to sound shocked. We're over twenty-one."

"Your parents will be so hurt!"

"My parents are somewhere in Alaska on vacation."

"What about Hunter's folks?"

"I told you things were dicey between Hunter and them. I doubt if this news will change anything."

"You know, Hunter asked me if I knew your family," Kate said. "He'd really wanted you to have them at the wedding."

"There'll be plenty of time for family," Jeannie said. "Especially with one the size of mine."

"No, I'm serious," said Kate. "He asked me a lot of questions when we were dancing at the reception." She narrowed her eyes comically. "It made me realize how much I don't know about you."

"There's not much to know," Jeannie said brightly. "I'm pretty dull, all things considered."

"Hunter doesn't think so."

"Wonderful," said Jeannie. "That means I'm doing something right." Maybe it was time to make a call....

"I CALLED MY PARENTS this afternoon," said Hunter over dinner that night.

Jeannie looked up from her salad. "I called my

parents this afternoon, too."

"What did yours say about the wedding?"

"They're still on vacation," said Jeannie. "My sister, however, was thrilled." And also concerned about Jeannie's lack of candor with Hunter. "How about your parents?"

"They extended their congratulations, asked about Daisy's health, then said they were off to play golf."

"You're kidding." She paused. "Aren't you?"

"The conversation took longer but that's all it amounted to." He cut into his chicken. "Now watch. They'll send us an arrangement of flowers with a balloon sticking out of it that says Congratulations." He met her eyes. "They like the personal touch."

"We'll send them wedding pictures," Jeannie said. "A big eight-by-ten glossy with Daisy in it. How could they resist?"

"Forget it," Hunter said, his tone sharp. "It's their loss. If they don't want to be part of our life, then I don't give a damn."

Jeannie couldn't help but regret that he was depriving Daisy of her grandparents' attentions, but then who was she to talk? The fact that they had made their calls without the other present was not lost on her. They each had their reasons but she found it very sad that it was Daisy who ultimately would pay the price.

THE FOLLOWING WEEK Hunter and Jeannie took Kate and Trey out for a thank-you dinner. One of Kate's friends, a registered nurse, was baby-sitting Daisy back at the apartment. Hunter chose a Hungarian restaurant in the East Seventies, a lush, old-world establishment with gas lamps and weeping violins and the best goulash in the city.

He was feeling particularly expansive that night. He'd been on fire at work, all the old ambition and drive he'd thought gone forever was back, burning hotter than ever. Without Daisy in the office to distract him, he was able to focus in on the tasks at hand and push through in record time. Knowing she was safe and secure at home with someone who loved her made all the difference.

Their marriage had been impulsive, crazy. But it was the smartest thing he'd ever done. The last few weeks had passed like scenes from a romantic movie. Bright sunny days. Warm passionate nights. All the time and space he needed to pursue his career.

A man couldn't ask for much more out of marriage.

"Look at them," Jeannie whispered to him between courses. She gestured toward Kate and Trey out on the dance floor. "They're crazy about each other. Look at the way they're gazing into each other's eyes."

"The last time I saw Trey like that he was photographing Miss January."

Jeannie gave him a poke in the ribs. "I'm serious, Hunter. There's romance in the air."

"You're right," he said, taking her hand. "From the first moment we met."

"Not exactly," said Jeannie with a rueful laugh.

"If I remember right, you had an eye on that blond model."

He gave her a blank stare. "Who?"

"Marcy," Jeannie prompted. "Tall, thin, big bo—".

"Oh, yeah. Marcy." His grin was infectious. "Now I remember."

"So do I," said Jeannie, "and I hope she's eating her heart out."

Trey and Kate returned from the dance floor.

Kate flashed them a cat-and-canary smile. "What were you two talking about over here?"

"None of your business," said Jeannie sweetly.

Kate glared at her in mock annoyance. "Fine," she said. "Keep your secrets. See if I care."

Everyone laughed. Nature abhorred a vacuum but not half as much as Kate hated secrets.

"Don't bug them, Katie," said Trey, still laughing. "Jeannie probably has another husband stashed away somewhere and they're—"

"Oh!" Jeannie leaped to her feet as ice water poured over the side of the table. "I can't believe I did that!" Her upended glass of water lay in the middle of the table.

She excused herself and ran to the ladies' room, praying Kate would stay where she was. *That was your guilty conscience reacting, Jeannie.*

"And what was that all about?" Kate asked as she burst through the ladies' room door a few moments later.

Jeannie blotted her skirt with a wad of paper towels. "I knocked over my water glass. It happens all the time."

"Not to you," Kate said. "What's wrong?"

"Nothing," she said brightly. "Find me a good blow dryer and we can get back inside."

SHE CAME TO HIM that night with a passion that left Hunter amazed.

She was everywhere, pleasuring, tempting, inviting him to lose himself in her and be found again and again.

"The lights," he said as she teased him with her lips and tongue. "I want to see you."

"Quiet." She placed her hand over his mouth. "No lights. No sound. Just let yourself feel."

He was a man accustomed to being in control, but when he tried to roll her over onto her back, his wife slipped just out of his reach.

"Tonight belongs to me," she said, letting the straps of her nightgown slip from her shoulders.

"Then let me—"

She moved in a way that stopped rational thought. His limber, inventive wife.

"I'm afraid you're going to give me trouble," she said, reaching for something on the nightstand beside her. He watched, blood pounding, as she slid a pair of silky black hose through her fingers.

His eyes narrowed as she drew closer.

"This is for your own good," she said, looping his wrists together with the filmy silk. "Trust me."

She branded him with her touch. He would know

her in the dark by the smell of her skin, the feel of her mouth against him. There was something urgent about her lovemaking, passion that went beyond heat and into pure fire. Slowly she moved her way up his body until she found his mouth with hers.

"Untie me," he said.

"Not yet." She dipped her head and took his nipple between her lips.

"Untie me," he repeated.

"Why?"

He told her exactly what he intended to do.

A voluptuous shiver rippled through her body.

With one quick movement he broke the fragile bonds that held him captive then pinned her to the bed with his body.

"I was right," she said. "You're dangerous."

He met her eyes. She smiled then opened herself to him, soul and body, and it was a very long time before they slept.

THAT NIGHT the dream returned. She had sensed its nearness, done her best to push it away, but still it found her, as she'd known it would.

The house sat on the corner of Maple Street and Hawthorne, a tiny Cape Cod with crisp black shutters and an air of happy domesticity about it. A huge pine wreath complete with red satin bow graced the front door and boughs of holly and twinkling lights decorated the windows and eaves.

It was everything Jeannie had ever wanted in life, every one of her girlhood dreams come true. This was the house she'd come to as a young bride, the place where her daughters had been conceived, the floors were the floors she and Dan had walked on those endless nights where nothing could ease a child's crying.

It was her home.

Christmas was three days away and there was so much still to be done that Jeannie despaired of finding the time. There were Barbie clothes to track down for the girls, the Fair Isle sweater to finish for Dan, the fishing pole for her dad and painter's easel for her mother, a slew of siblings and nieces and nephews to shop for and—

"Cookies!" She sat up in bed, heart pounding. Good grief, she hadn't even bought the ingredients yet. She glanced at the clock on the nightstand: 5:00 a.m. Who in their right mind would be thinking about cookies at that hour?

Jeannie knew the answer to that. She climbed from bed, careful not to wake her sleeping husband and reached for her bathrobe. Any mother with only seventy-two hours left until Christmas morning, that's who.

She padded downstairs to check the pantry for supplies. There was no sense trying to sleep. She wouldn't be able to close her eyes now that she remembered that the holiday cookies weren't even in the planning stages yet. She'd make a list, slip into her clothes, then race out to the store and be back before her family stirred.

"Up early, Jeannie," said Ethel, the night cashier

at Brody's Cash 'n' Carry a few miles away. "Got the Christmas crazies?"

"Show me a woman who doesn't and I'll show you a Grinch," Jeannie said, rummaging through her pocketbook for her wallet. She'd spent more time in the store than she'd expected—and more money as well. But didn't everyone come Christmastime? "I have to go home and bake ten dozen cookies for the hungry hordes."

"Save me a pfefferneuse," said Ethel with a friendly grin. "Nobody makes 'em like you do."

Jeannie eased the station wagon slowly out of the snowy parking lot, wishing for the hundredth time that they could afford a four-wheel drive. Maybe someday, she told herself as she made her way home. Living in northern Minnesota gave you a profound respect for Mother Nature. Ice and snow and bitter winter winds that—

She tilted her head to one side. Sirens at that hour of the morning? The town's noon whistle had the disconcerting habit of going off whenever it darn well felt like it. She grinned and continued driving. Back home Dan must be grumbling right now and pulling the pillow over his ears to drown out the sound.

Instead of fading the sound of the whistle intensified. A fire, she wondered as she neared the foot of Hawthorne. Every year the local paper ran heartbreaking stories about deadly holiday fires and Jeannie had always whispered a quick prayer that her own loved ones were safe from harm.

And that was when she saw it. Billows of black

smoke racing toward the morning clouds. Angry tongues of flame hissing through the cold air.

Fire engines. Powerful jets of water racing against the inevitable. The red-rimmed eyes of volunteer firemen as she ran toward her home that was no longer there—

HER SCREAM split the stillness of the room.

"What the hell—?" Hunter sat bolt upright in bed. Jeannie was tangled in the sheets, eyes closed, trapped inside a nightmare of frightening proportions.

Her voice shook with terror. "Let me go! Don't try to stop me!"

"Jeannie." He gripped her by the shoulders and shook her gently. "Jeannie, wake up."

She twisted away from him, eyes open now but unseeing. "No! Let me go! The fire...they can't breathe...they—"

He shook her harder this time. Sweat beaded at her temples. Her breathing was shallow, erratic.

His adrenaline pumped in response.

"You're dreaming, Jeannie. It's only a dream. You're safe...you're with me."

He forced her to look at him, to really see him.

"Everyone's safe, Jeannie. You...me...Daisy."

She drew a long, shuddering breath. "Hunter." She sagged against him, body limp with exhaustion. "Oh, God."

He held her in his arms, stroking her silky hair, murmuring to her as her trembling eased.

"That was one hell of a nightmare," he said after a while.

She sat up in bed, touching her throat and wincing. "Did I scream?"

He nodded. "You screamed."

Her eyes closed for an instant. "Did I wake Daisy?"

"She's sleeping like a baby."

Jeannie managed a shaky smile. "You do have a way with words, Hunter."

"Are you okay?"

"Just embarrassed." She glanced toward the window. "Did I—did I say anything?"

He hesitated, unsure about the right thing to do. Did you confront nightmares or forget them? He opted instead for the truth. "You were calling for help."

"For myself?"

"No. It sounded like someone was trapped in a fire. It's just a dream," he said, pulling her close to him.

"I'm sorry," she said. "I feel like such an idiot. Grown women don't have nightmares."

"Don't," he said. "Everyone has bad dreams now and then. Forget about it."

Her head drooped against his chest and he held her close until she fell asleep, wishing he could banish her fears—whatever they might be.

"YOUR PARENTS sound great," Hunter said a few nights later as he put down the letter they'd sent, congratulating the newlyweds on their marriage.

"They are great," said Jeannie, feeding Daisy a spoonful of baby glop. "The older I get, the more I appreciate how terrific they are."

"Why don't we fly out to Minnesota to see them next week after they get home?" Her parents were currently up in Alaska on their annual vacation.

"They'd love that," she said after a moment. "Maybe around Thanksgiving would be better." She smiled as she wiped Daisy's mouth and Daisy smiled back. She looked over at Hunter. "They do it up big at the inn. Lots of harvest colors, hayrides for the kids, bobbing for apples—the whole all-American thing in spades."

"Why wait until Thanksgiving?" he asked. "There's no time like the present."

"A man who's anxious to meet his in-laws. You're one of a kind, Hunter."

He chuckled as Daisy wrinkled her nose at the taste of zucchini. "So what do you say? Next weekend. We could fly out on Friday and be back Sunday night."

"I'll call them when they get home and we'll see about arranging something."

He started to push again but caught himself. This was his marriage, not a business deal. He had to learn to give as well as take. It was hard, but he thought he was learning.

There were times he felt as if he were seeing the world for the first time, as if Jeannie had opened up his heart to feelings he'd believed existed only in other people's hearts.

Lately, though, he'd had the feeling that there was something else going on below the glossy surface of their life together. It was nothing he could explain, just the sense that nothing this good could stay that way forever. Now and again there was a shadow around Jeannie, a subtle shift in mood that made him wonder about the woman he'd married. Neither one of them went in for philosophizing or dredging up past lives and past sins. They had come together to share the present and look forward to the future. The past was yesterday's news.

Still, the sense that she was more complicated than she appeared lingered. Another man might have held her in his arms and asked questions. He was content simply to hold her.

His live-for-today philosophy had served him well in life. Shrugging off excess emotional baggage made it easier to climb the ladder in business. Callie had never been able to do that, however. She'd been the changeling in the family, the one who went through life with her defenses down, eager to see and feel and experience everything the world had to offer. She'd kept scores of journals in her attempt to wring all the best from life. Hunter had them locked in the credenza in his office. He'd never even cracked one volume.

He had everything he'd ever wanted. His career was working on all cylinders. He had the time and the space to pursue his goals. Callie's daughter grew stronger and brighter every day. And he had the woman of his wildest fantasies in his bed with him each night.

Only a fool would look for trouble.

KATE AND Jeannie had a running date for a girls-only luncheon on the second Saturday of each month. Hunter laughed when his wife interpreted that invitation to include Daisy now as well.

"I don't think the folks at the Russian Tea Room would appreciate Daisy's unique charm," he said as he watched Jeannie dress. She made the act seem downright erotic. "I'll take care of her. You and Kate have a good time."

She kissed them both goodbye and raced out the door in a cloud of Chanel No. 5. Her footsteps had barely faded before he found himself fighting the urge to race after her.

A long time ago he'd shared a week in the Bahamas with a model named Khrystyne. Every time she left to do some shopping, he'd found himself basking in the luxury of having the hotel room to himself. The peace. The quiet. The privacy.

A pretty good indication a relationship was doomed, now that he thought about it.

Not this time, however. The door had barely closed behind his bride, and already he was counting the hours until she returned.

"I've got it bad, Daisy," he said, carting the baby back into the living room where he'd set up a play area for her. He loved the sound of his wife's laughter, the smell of her skin, the way she made every day seem special just by being in his life.

He settled Daisy down on her play mat then settled himself down at the desk to draft a proposal for an ad campaign Grantham expected to see in perfect condition by Wednesday. Hunter had no doubt at all that he would knock Grantham's argyles right off.

AT LUNCH Kate kept Jeannie laughing from borscht through blinis. One of the Cossack-clad waiters was an underemployed stand-up comic, same as Kate, and he spent as much time with them as he could, trading stories and helping to keep Jeannie in stitches.

"You realize Madonna got her start as a hatcheck girl here," said Kate as they left the restaurant. "Maybe I should rethink my career path."

"Your career path is fine," said Jeannie. "It's going to happen big for you one day soon." She gave her friend a hug. "Just you wait and see."

"How about you?" asked Kate as they headed back toward their neighborhood. "When do you get back to work?"

Jeannie shuddered. "Don't even talk about it. I have that Hawaii job coming up the end of the week and I can't even bring myself to remind Hunter."

"Better get moving, girl," said Kate. "Most men don't care for surprises like that."

They stopped in front of a pricey jewelry store and admired a diamond ring neither could afford.

"To tell you the truth," said Jeannie, "I've been thinking of calling Leah Peretti to fill in for me." If she was going to do so she'd better hurry. The trip was set for next week.

"On a trip to Maui?" Kate pressed a palm to Jeannie's forehead. "You're in worse shape than I thought."

"Maui doesn't compare to what I've got at home, Kate."

"So take them with you. Let Hunter play help-meet for a change."

Jeannie gave her friend a sharp look. "And what's that supposed to mean?"

"Not what you think," said Kate. "It's just you have a career, too. Don't let it fall by the wayside because you got married. I don't know if anyone's told you, but this isn't the 1950s."

Jeannie smiled. How could Kate understand how much home and family meant to her? There was nothing on earth to compare to the happiness she felt each morning when she woke up knowing she had Hunter and Daisy in her life.

They said goodbye at the corner of Fifth Avenue and Sixty-fifth Street. Kate had a rehearsal to get to and, Jeannie suspected, Trey Whittaker would figure somehow in her evening plans.

She headed north on Fifth Avenue, feeling sublimely happy.

The only dark cloud on the horizon was of her own making and even that she could banish if she chose to.

Maybe the time had come to tell Hunter about the family she'd lost. She was tired of brushing away ghosts, of willing away shadows. Once she told him, she'd be able to let the past take its rightful place in her memory. Angie had been right when she said Jeannie owed it to him. And, more importantly, she owed it to herself.

Happiness was right there in the palm of her hand and this time it wasn't going to slip away.

THE WORK was going well. The words were there when he needed them and they were witty and clever and destined to make Green Grass Lawn Tractors the hottest thing on wheels since the Ferrari Testarossa.

He was about to pour himself a beer and admire his handiwork when the intercom buzzed.

"Mr. Phillips." Bill's friendly voice crackled over the intercom. "A Mr. Burnett is here to see you."

"Burnett?" He couldn't think of any Burnetts in his Rolodex. "What's it about?"

"He says it's personal."

"Okay, Bill. Send him up." Burnett...Burnett. Offhand he couldn't come up with a face to fit the name but that was no reason for the odd prickle of apprehension working its way up his spine.

He opened the door at the first knock. A tall, handsome man of middle age smiled at him.

"Duncan Burnett." A definite Scottish brogue.

"Hunter Phillips." He extended his hand. The guy had a good grip. Strong without being obnoxious.

They stood there looking at each other.

"Do we know each other?" Hunter asked.

"In a way."

Hunter waited.

Apprehension gave way to full-blown fear.

"You're Callie Phillips's brother, aren't you?"

Hunter's gut twisted and, involuntarily, he glanced toward the baby playing innocently on the living-room floor.

He opened the door wide and trouble walked right in.

"'AFTERNOON, Mrs. Phillips." Bill the doorman tipped his hat to her as she stepped into the cool lobby.

"Isn't it a wonderful afternoon, Bill?" she asked. "Just the best ever."

"I buzzed in a friend of your husband's a minute ago," he said jovially. "If you hurry up, you might catch him by the elevator."

"Thanks, Bill."

Trey, she thought as she made her way across the lobby. The love bug had found itself a willing victim and Trey Whittaker needed advice on how to woo the wary Kate.

She rounded the corner just in time to see a tall, fair-haired man disappear into the elevator. It wasn't Trey. A knot of apprehension formed in her stomach.

"Don't be ridiculous," she whispered. It was probably one of the execs from C V & S, bringing over some papers for Hunter to look at. Saturdays meant nothing to ad men.

The elevator took forever to return to the lobby. She stepped into the car and pressed the button to close the doors. Her keys jangled from her fingers as she exited on the fifteenth floor then hurried down the hall to their apartment.

She was being ridiculous. There wasn't a thing in the world to worry about. She'd had a great time with Kate this afternoon, but the best part of all was coming home to her husband, their child—

And a strange man sitting in the middle of their living room with Daisy on his lap.

Chapter Nine

Jeannie stood inside the doorway, arms wrapped tightly across her chest. Her eyes darted past Hunter to Burnett. The Scotsman held Daisy stiffly, the way Hunter had in the beginning. He felt as if he were seeing himself as he'd been almost nine months ago, awkward and uncertain and out of his depth.

Yet, all Hunter had to do was take one look at the Scotsman and Daisy together and he knew everything he needed to know without asking a single question.

From the look on his wife's face, so did Jeannie.

He crossed the room to where she stood. "Jeannie," he said, placing a hand on her shoulder, "this is Duncan Burnett."

Awkwardly Burnett tried to hold Daisy and rise to his feet simultaneously. Jeannie leaped forward and took the baby from him.

"He wouldn't have dropped her, Jeannie." Hunter's voice sounded tight and unnatural to his ears.

"I think your wife correctly gauged the situation,"

Burnett said with easy grace. "Daisy is quite a handful, Mrs. Phillips."

"Jeannie," she said automatically then looked toward Hunter.

"Duncan was a friend of Callie's." If she was looking for more, he was afraid he couldn't provide it.

Her sharp intake of breath didn't go unnoticed. Daisy looked up at her curiously. "Did—did you know Hunter's sister well?"

An odd look passed across Burnett's regular features. "We were good friends."

Jeannie seemed to cling to the words as if they were a life preserver.

Hunter, however, had no such illusions. "Duncan and Callie knew each other in Tokyo."

"Well," she said, holding Daisy more tightly. "How long will you be in town?"

"Two days," Burnett said.

She nodded, looking toward Hunter to break the awkward silence.

"I've asked Duncan to join us for dinner."

"It's only leftovers," she said to the Scotsman. "With all the wonderful restaurants in this city, I'm sure you could do much better."

Burnett's gaze flickered from Hunter to Jeannie. "While I appreciate the offer, I'm afraid I have other plans."

He was a perceptive man.

Maybe too perceptive.

Burnett turned again to Hunter. "Perhaps we can

continue this tomorrow at the hotel. I'll have the pictures ready for you." He nodded to them both. "I'll see myself out."

Jeannie settled Daisy back down on her play mat. "Wh-what was that all about?" she asked as the door closed behind the man.

She deserved the truth. "I think he's Daisy's father."

Her face grew pale. "You asked him?"

"No, but it was pretty obvious."

"So what if they had the same coloring," she said, her voice higher than normal. "That doesn't mean he's Daisy's father."

"Then why was he here, Jeannie?" he asked, feeling as if he'd gone fifteen rounds with the heavyweight champion. "He didn't stop by for a game of cards."

"He heard about your sister's death," Jeannie said, her jaw settling into a stubborn line. "What did he say—he had some pictures of her? That's all it was."

"He wants Daisy." In a bizarre way, it felt good to say the words, to drag them out of the shadows. "He—"

"She's *yours*, Hunter," she broke in. "You raised her. She's your daughter."

"She's not my daughter."

"In all the ways that matter, she is."

"Except one." He looked at Daisy, as a kaleidoscope of emotions twisted through him. "If he's Daisy's father, we'll have to deal with it."

"If your sister had wanted him to be part of Daisy's life, she would have married him."

"Come on, Jeannie," he said. "This isn't getting us anywhere." He glanced toward Daisy then looked away. Sharp words were flying over her head like knives, but she sat there playing with her plastic keys, as secure and happy as she'd ever been. "If Burnett's her father, he has the right to raise his own daughter the way he sees fit."

"For God's sake, Hunter!" Jeannie exploded. "You sound like an article in a women's magazine. This is real life we're talking about. This is *Daisy!*"

Daisy looked up at the sound of her name. "Dah!"

"That's you," said Jeannie, voice breaking. "You might not know it, but she does."

"She's a baby," he said, looking away. "She can't talk yet. Those are only sounds."

"You're a fool, Hunter. The truth is staring you right in the face, but you're too blind to see it." She bent down and pressed a kiss to the top of the baby's golden head. "This isn't about Burnett at all, is it? It's about you."

"The hell it is." He didn't like the direction the argument was taking. Emotional issues had never been his strong suit. When it came to talk of feelings, he was as inarticulate as Daisy.

"I don't know why I didn't realize it sooner," Jeannie said, pacing the room. "It's so clear to me now. You've finally found your way out."

"Drop it, Jeannie." His voice was low, deadly calm.

"You don't know how to handle this. You can't admit you love that little girl and don't want to lose her."

The muscles in his jaw tightened. A wiser woman might have noticed.

"That's it," she continued. "It's easier to let some stranger walk in here and stake a claim than it is to admit that she's your daughter."

"It doesn't matter what I think," Hunter said through clenched teeth. "If Burnett's her father, the next step is his."

"And you'll just let her go?"

"I'll let her go."

Her beautiful blue eyes filled with tears. "You're lying, Hunter. You couldn't possibly mean that."

"What do you want me to say, Jeannie? That I don't care about Daisy, that things would be easier if she wasn't around? If that's what you want to hear, tell me and I'll say it."

"Tell me you'll fight for her," she said. "Tell me you'll keep our family together."

HUNTER TURNED AWAY and said nothing. Jeannie watched as he walked toward the window and looked down at the street. She thought her heart would break against the unfairness of it all. *I can't go through it again,* she thought, wishing she could go to him, hold him, convince him to open his heart to happiness. *I can't bear to lose another family....*

But Burnett's arrival had changed everything. Neither she nor Hunter could look at their impulsive marriage in quite the same way again. They'd been playing house this past month, as if their situation was your average, everyday American love story.

Only thing was, nobody had ever mentioned that one very important word: love. They loved Daisy and pizza and the way they fit together in bed. She had freed Hunter to get on with his career, while he and Daisy had given Jeannie the family she'd yearned for.

But beyond that neither one of them had dared to go.

And now she was afraid it was too late.

Talk to me, Hunter. Maybe together we can find a way....

THE SILENCE in the room was palpable. It had form and shape and weight, and Hunter knew if he touched her all hell would break loose. The argument had set up a barrier between them, as real as a brick wall, although it couldn't be seen with the naked eye.

Women needed words to soothe the pain. He knew Jeannie was waiting for him to say something, anything, to bridge the gap between them that was growing wider with each second that ticked past.

He wanted to touch his wife, stroke her, make love to her—tell her what he was thinking in the oldest way possible. Find his own comfort in her softness and warmth. The words she needed to hear weren't part of his vocabulary and maybe they never would be.

SOMETIMES SILENCE SAID more than words ever could.

Hunter grabbed some leftover chicken and a can of

soda from the refrigerator then buried himself in paperwork.

Daisy seemed oblivious to the mounting tension in the apartment. The baby ate her dinner with enthusiasm then laughed and splashed her way through bath time.

Jeannie, however, felt as if she would break apart any second, shattering into a thousand pieces.

"I'm putting Daisy to bed," she said from the entrance to the living room.

He didn't look up from the stack of papers before him. "I'll be there in a minute."

She wanted to shake him until his teeth rattled. He loved that baby the way a parent loved his child, only he was too stubborn and scared to admit it, not even to himself. He had every right to fight for Daisy but she wasn't certain he had the heart. Her husband liked the easy way and there was nothing easy or pleasant about what lay ahead of them if Burnett wanted to fight.

This beautiful little girl with her cornflower-blue eyes and sweet disposition could be snatched away from them in the blink of an eye and apparently Hunter was going to do nothing to stop it from happening.

You knew what he was about when you married him. Ambitious. Sometimes opportunistic. Pushy and opinionated and destined for the fast lane at C V & S. He'd told her himself that he'd hated the idea of a child. Was it any wonder he had resisted the notion that Daisy was now his daughter? Now that he had the chance to pass Daisy on to someone else, he was painfully eager to do so.

On their wedding day Walter Grantham had congratulated Hunter for being smart enough to marry a woman who worked with babies for a living. Now that Jeannie was around, he'd said, Hunter would be able to focus his attentions back on his work where they belonged.

Maybe there had been more truth to that statement than Jeannie had been willing to admit.

He wasn't anything like her first husband, a man who'd been happy with his lot in life, satisfied with a wife and two little girls and his small plot of Minnesota land. Dan hadn't asked for much from life, but he'd always considered himself the richest man in the world. "I've got you three girls," he'd always said to Jeannie and his daughters. "I can't ask for anything more."

Hunter dreamed big. He'd been on his own for a long time. He thrived on ambition and competition, all the things Dan had hated. Hunter was complicated, difficult, impossible to understand and somehow she loved him with all her heart.

She sank into the rocking chair next to the crib and watched as Daisy drifted off into sleep. For a second she saw her own little girls in that crib, but the image vanished as quickly as it had appeared. The here and now was all that was important. It was all anyone really had.

And now it was slipping away.

"Is she asleep?" Hunter asked, appearing in the doorway.

Jeannie nodded, unable to speak around the lump in her throat.

He leaned into the crib, laying his forefinger against Daisy's tiny cheek. The gesture touched something deep inside her heart and she hated herself for having believed the kind of happiness she'd known this past month could last.

"You look tired," he said. "You should get some sleep."

"I will."

He started to say something more and her breath caught. *Tell me you'll fight for her, Hunter. Tell me nothing matters more than our family—or more than being together.* Tears sprang to her eyes and she looked down, blinking rapidly. *Tell me you love me.*

"Jeannie, I—" He stopped abruptly.

Please, Hunter...we can find a way together, the three of us....

"I'm going out," he said after a moment. "I don't know when I'll be back."

"We'll come with you."

He shook his head. "This is something I have to do alone."

"You're going to see Burnett, aren't you?"

He didn't answer. But then, he didn't need to. She could feel his answer in every bone in her body.

WALKING OUT on Jeannie and Daisy was the hardest thing Hunter had ever done.

The look of pain in Jeannie's eyes followed him as

he rode down the elevator, walked with him across the lobby, then haunted him as he stepped out onto the street. From the very beginning she'd been able to see past his defenses, straight through to the heart he'd never believed he possessed.

He'd felt Jeannie's eyes on him as he leaned over the crib to say good-night to Daisy. The sight of that beautiful, sleeping baby had torn at him like the slash of a knife but he'd managed to keep his expression bland, his emotions under control—at least, outwardly.

Jeannie loved Daisy as if she were her own. Every touch, every gesture radiated love in its purest sense. Callie had given birth to Daisy but in every other way Jeannie was her mother.

He understood that. He'd accepted it.

Why then had it taken him so long to understand what that baby girl meant to him?

When Burnett had shown up on the doorstep that afternoon, Hunter's first instinct had been to slam the door shut in his face.

"I should've," he muttered as he strode down the street. Or landed a left hook to his jaw. Something.

But he'd opened the door wide, set Daisy on the guy's lap—if Jeannie hadn't walked in when she did, he might have packed up the baby's belongings and sent her on her way.

For months he'd told anyone who asked that he wasn't Daisy's father, that her "real" father was somewhere out there. *The kid can do better than me,*

he'd said more than once. He was the guy who'd
thought projectile vomiting was part of Desert Storm.
He'd learned a hell of a lot in short order, but the
feeling that he was shortchanging Daisy had never left
him, not even for a minute. When he saw Burnett it
had all rushed in on him with the force of a sudden
storm.

The shortcomings. The mistakes.

The way Daisy had opened up his heart to love.

Without that little girl in his life, the happiness he'd
found with Jeannie would have been impossible. He
hadn't understood a damn thing about love or families
or all the other things everyone else took for granted.

It had taken a baby girl with cornflower-blue eyes
to show him the secret of being happy.

He'd been so caught up in his own concerns that
he might not have noticed paradise—not even when
it was staring him in the face.

And so there he was again. Still scared. Still angry.
Only this time it wasn't because he wanted to shrug
off responsibility the way you shrugged off an old
coat. It was because he might lose everything in life
that really mattered.

Daisy was his flesh and blood.

And Jeannie was the woman he loved.

They were worth fighting for. Worth putting himself on the line to hold fast. This was the secret his
sister had always known, that you had to climb out
on a limb in order to reach the sweetest fruit.

And if sometimes you fell, it was a chance you had
to take.

He stepped out into the street and hailed a cab.

"The Westbury Hotel," he said as the driver gunned the engine.

To hell with waiting until tomorrow morning. It was time to climb out onto that limb and take his chances.

WHEN THE TELEPHONE rang Jeannie was on it in an instant.

"Jeannie, it's Taylor from Kramer Booking. Haven't you checked your messages, girl? I've been going ballistic trying to track you down."

Jeannie glanced at the clock. "It's almost midnight, Taylor. This'd better be good." *Hunter, where are you? This was supposed to be you on the telephone.*

"Remember that courier pouch we sent you last week? Well, dust it off and get your butt to the airport. We're calling up the troops *stat.*"

"You've got to be kidding, Taylor. The sixteenth is still a week away."

"Forget the sixteenth. There's a push to get the spot on air in time for the first sweeps week."

"I can't just pick up on a moment's notice."

"Neither can anybody else," said Taylor, "but they're all on their way to the airport. You did sign a contract for a two-week stint."

"You're going to play hardball?"

"Absolutely."

There was nothing holding her here. Even if a miracle happened and Hunter claimed Daisy as his own,

she knew her own secrets would destroy their last
chance for happiness.

Kate would be willing to come over and watch
Daisy until Hunter came home. Maybe a clean break
was the smartest thing to do.

"Send a car for me," she told Taylor. "I'll be
ready to go in fifteen minutes."

BURNETT OPENED the door at Hunter's first knock.

And it was a good thing because Hunter's adrenaline was pumping so hard and fast that he would
have kicked in the door at the slightest provocation.

"A bit late for visiting, isn't it, Phillips?" The
damn Scotsman managed to look sophisticated in his
bathrobe.

Hunter stepped into the foyer. "Daisy's mine," he
said, staring Burnett in the eye. "She's my daughter,
and if you think you're going to take her away from
me, you're in for the fight of your life."

Burnett closed the door. "I don't know about
you," he said, heading toward the sitting room, "but
I need a drink."

"I didn't come here for a friendly shot, Burnett."
Hunter followed him into the room. "I want to talk
about my daughter."

Burnett grabbed two tumblers from the bar then
poured three fingers of Scotch into each.

"Callie told me you were volatile," Burnett said,
handing a tumbler to Hunter.

"Yeah?" he said. "She didn't tell me anything
about you."

Burnett lifted his glass. "To Callie."

Hunter nodded, eyes burning. "To my sister."

The two men gulped down some Scotch then squared off once again.

"Okay," said Hunter, putting down the glass. "Great hospitality. Now let's get down to business." He met Burnett's eyes—and saw Daisy in them. He didn't want to, but there was no avoiding it. "You're Daisy's father."

"Her *biological* father."

Hunter blinked. Was he the last person on earth to understand the difference?

"You knocked up my sister, then walked out on her."

"If I wasn't reasonably sure you would best me, I'd call you out for that, Phillips."

The two men glared at each other across the room.

"Callie wanted a child," Burnett said. "She knew the risks but her desire for a baby outweighed them in her eyes."

"And you accommodated her."

Burnett's expression softened. "There was a great deal of affection between us," he said, "and we both understood the boundaries of our relationship."

Hunter listened impassively to the story. "That's all terrific," he said at last, "but that doesn't tell me why you showed up on my doorstep."

Burnett seemed to age right in front of Hunter. "I wanted to see her," he said. "Just once."

"And now that you've seen her—?"

Burnett's shrug was eloquent. For an instant Hunter

pitied him. "I get on with my life," he said in his Scottish burr, "and you get on with yours."

"How do I know you won't show up again one day and want to turn Daisy's life upside down?"

Burnett reached into the briefcase that rested on the Louis XIV chair near the bar. He withdrew a sheaf of papers then handed them to Hunter.

"Medical records going back two generations. Genealogy information." His smile was weary. "And a signed document releasing all claim on your beautiful little daughter."

"JEANNIE!" Hunter exploded into the apartment a little after seven in the morning, bearing bagels, cream cheese, and a split of champagne. "Rise and shine! Grab Daisy and let's do some celebrating!"

"Hi, Hunter."

He whirled around to see Kate Mullen standing in the doorway to the kitchen.

"Where's Jeannie?" he asked, glancing around the apartment.

"She said to tell you that Taylor called. They moved the shoot up a few days."

"Hawaii?"

Kate nodded. "That's the one."

He'd almost forgotten about that. Somehow he'd never imagined she would leave them.

"It was an emergency," Kate said, obviously uncomfortable. "They had her signed contract and all."

"Maybe I can catch her at the airport."

"Too late. She took off from Newark ten minutes ago."

Jeannie had called Kate to come over and watch Daisy until Hunter came home. He knew Kate had to be wondering what in hell he'd been doing wandering the streets on a Saturday night. Not exactly the behavior of your average newlywed.

As soon as Kate left he headed into Daisy's room. "Daah!" she said as he approached the crib. "Daah!" She waved her arms and legs in the air, gurgling with delight as he lifted her into his arms. One chubby hand touched his cheek and came away wet.

"No apologies, Daise," he said, holding her close to his chest, breathing in her sweet baby smell. "Your old man's got a lot to be happy about this morning."

She was his little girl. His daughter. The signed documents from Burnett only confirmed what he already knew in his heart.

Still, something was missing. He wasn't just Daisy's father, he was part of a family. A family that included Jeannie.

Carrying Daisy, he prowled around the apartment, sure Jeannie must have left a note for him somewhere. Even a go-to-hell note. Anything was better than this uneasy feeling that he'd come home a lot later than he thought.

"She'll probably call this evening," he said to Daisy as he fed his daughter her breakfast.

Soon as she landed in Hawaii.

HE SAT AND STARED at the telephone all day. Once he called the operator just to see if the damn thing was working.

"Your telephone is fine, sir. Have a good day."

"What do you know?" he mumbled, hanging up the phone. The phone company hadn't been the same since they broke up Ma Bell into a group of bouncing Baby Bells.

Not even a wrong number.

Okay. He wasn't going to get crazy about it. Twelve-hour flights could do a real number on your body clock. Besides, he knew all about location shoots. They probably met her at the airport with a fast-food hamburger and a shooting script that would increase by leaps and bounds as the days went on.

She'd settle in.

Catch up on her sleep.

And then she'd call.

E.T. had called home. So would his wife.

BY WEDNESDAY even Hunter had to admit that Jeannie wasn't going to call.

Twice he dialed Kate's number, determined to ask her for the name of his wife's hotel on Maui but male pride stopped him each time. He was her husband. He was supposed to know things like that.

It seemed as if Daisy had cried nonstop since Jeannie left on Sunday morning. If he didn't know better he'd swear all thirty-two teeth were coming in at once. He held her, fed her, did all the things he'd always done for her, but it wasn't enough. "You want

Jeannie, don't you, Daise?'' he said as he walked the floor with his little girl. "You're not the only one.''

He could handle the cooking and cleaning as well as he ever did. He could hire a nanny with references a mile long to care for Daisy. But there was no substitute for the sweet warmth of the woman you loved.

"I'm distressed,'' said Walter Grantham on Thursday afternoon. "That proposal was below standard.''

"I'm working on it,'' said Hunter. "I'm redoing the storyboard. Ed Fisk likes the changes.''

Grantham's gaze rested on Daisy who was asleep in her office playpen. "I see you have a visitor.''

Hunter nodded, but made no comment.

"Is this going to be a permanent thing?''

In the real world, people married and had kids. Too bad Grantham only saw them as potential consumers. "She won't be doing her graduate work here, if that's what you're worried about.''

Grantham had never been one for humor. "I hope when your wife returns, she'll resume her duties and the child can stay home where she belongs.''

"My wife doesn't have duties, Walter.''

"No offense, Phillips. It just seemed to me you had a sweet deal going there. You've done some of your best work since the nuptials.''

Keep your mouth shut, a warning voice sounded. *You can't afford to lose your job over some stupid remark.*

Grantham, however, was on a roll. Hunter's eyes glazed over as Grantham waxed nostalgic for the good old days when a woman knew her place.

"…the White Orchid is too rich for our blood," Grantham was saying when Hunter tuned in again. "I don't know where the competition's getting the money but—"

"The White Orchid?" Hunter snapped to attention. "That fancy hotel in Maui?"

Grantham looked at him strangely. "The hotel where your wife is, Phillips. Haven't you been listening?"

Hunter started throwing papers into his briefcase then packing away Daisy's stuff in the duffel that doubled as a diaper bag. "I'm going to need some time off," he said, slipping into his jacket. "A week. Maybe two."

"You're joking, aren't you?" Grantham's tone implied Hunter had better be.

"Do I look like I'm joking?"

"I don't know what's going on, but we can't have anarchy at C V & S."

Hunter continued packing up his stuff. "I'll fax you the revised proposal. If you have any messages, use electronic mail." He bent down to pick up Daisy. "I'll be in touch."

"Walk out that door, Hunter, and you might not have a job to come back to."

"I'll take my chances."

Grantham was sputtering with outrage. Sooner or later there would be hell to pay for this stunt, but it didn't much matter to Hunter.

All that mattered was finding Jeannie before it was too late.

Chapter Ten

"I'm afraid we're going to be here in L.A. for quite a while," the flight attendant apologized as Hunter gathered up Daisy's things.

"Any guesses?" asked Hunter.

"Four hours definite. Six hours likely. If you're leaving the airport, make sure you call for information each hour."

"What next?" he muttered as he scooped up his daughter.

Of course he could have waited until tomorrow afternoon to catch a nice, cushy first-class seat on a *non*stop from New York to Honolulu, but once he knew where Jeannie was, nothing could stop him, not even stopovers in L.A.

Juggling duffel, overnight bag, and Daisy, he exited the jetway. He felt as if he'd just finished last in a triathlon. Daisy, however, was inordinately cheerful. She probably knew they were on their way to find Jeannie.

"What happened to all the crying you've been doing?" he asked as they headed toward the lounge.

"Daah!" she said, tugging at his ear.

"Old material, Daisy. How about trying something new?"

The flight attendants had fawned all over Daisy, cooing about what a terrific little traveler she was. Why not, thought Hunter. After all, how many kids log eleven thousand miles before they're fourteen days old the way Daisy had?

Daisy seemed perfectly content to play with her plastic keys in the airport lounge but Hunter couldn't settle down. Maybe it was his mood. Maybe it was the fact that for months he'd been living at the outer edge of control.

Or maybe it was just time.

He rented a sedan and a car seat for Daisy then set out for his parents' condo on the beach.

"HUNTER." His mother's polite smile widened just a little bit. "Won't you come in?"

He had to hand it to the woman. If she was surprised at seeing him on her doorstep for the first time in three years, it didn't show.

"Fred," she called out. "We have guests."

His father bustled into the foyer with that self-important air peculiar to most new retirees. "Well," he said, shaking Hunter's hand. "Well, well, well." He reached around Daisy for the bags. "Let me take your things."

"And what brings you here?" asked his mother as she ushered him into the living room.

"I had a few hours to kill between planes."

His father peered out the front window. "And where is your lovely new wife? Is she parking the car?"

"Jeannie is in Hawaii." He pointed toward Daisy who was sitting on his lap watching her grandparents with wide-eyed interest. "We're on our way to meet her."

Their collective gaze flickered over Daisy, held for an instant, then flickered away.

His mother fluttered around, offering him unsalted cashews, trail mix, or a club sandwich.

"Nothing, Mom," he said. "I'm fine."

"A drink," said his father. "Scotch on the rocks."

"I'm driving," said Hunter. "I wouldn't mind some iced tea...and some juice for Daisy." He reached into his duffel and extracted a bottle. "This one's clean."

"Is there—is there any particular juice she likes?" asked his mother, her gaze again lingering on her baby granddaughter.

"Apple," he said. "That's her favorite."

His mother's practiced smile slipped for a moment and became real. "Just like Callie when she was that age."

There. She'd said it. The ice had been broken.

His father, however, leaped in to patch up the damage. "So tell me about your flight," he boomed, sitting on the couch opposite Hunter and Daisy. "Did you take one of those new air buses they're so crazy about in Europe? Don't care too much for them myself. Give me a good old Boeing 747 anyday. Good enough for the space shuttle and it's good enough for me.''

His parents' impersonal chatter had never much bothered him. He'd grown up with their abridged view of the world and accepted it for what it was. Today, however, it was driving him right up the wall.

Damn it, but he wanted more. Living with Jeannie, he had begun to see a better way. You could be happy in life. *Really* happy. Not just biding your time until they put you in the ground. He and Jeannie hadn't begun to scratch the surface with each other but at least they had the excuse of knowing each other less than two months.

He'd known his parents all his life and he still had no idea what made them tick.

His mother hurried in with iced tea and the juice. She handed him the bottle. *This is Callie's daughter,* he thought as he gave the bottle to Daisy. *This is all you have left of the baby you carried forty years ago. Are you going to let this opportunity slip away without even holding her in your arms?*

He showed them a picture of Jeannie on their wedding day and they made the appropriate comments. To his own amazement, the whole story of Duncan Burnett and Jeannie's escape to Hawaii came pouring out. They weren't the kind of parents who were comfortable with any degree of emotion, and there he was spilling his guts for all to see.

But then again up until last month he hadn't been all that different, had he? Keeping life at a distance, safe behind a screen. He'd accepted his beautiful wife at face value and never once tried to discover who lived behind it.

He glanced at his watch. "I'd better shove off pretty soon. I don't want to miss the flight."

His mother started to say something but stopped abruptly. He saw the way her attention was riveted to the beautiful little girl on his lap. Did she see the resemblance to her own little girl? Did his parents have any idea what they were missing by turning away from their granddaughter?

"Can I call the airport?" he asked.

"Use the kitchen phone," said his mother. "Near the pantry door."

He seated Daisy on a nest of cushions and headed for the kitchen.

When he came back into the living room his father had the baby on his lap. His father's hazel eyes were glistening but that could have been the reflection of the sun on his glasses.

Hunter picked up his duffel. "I'd better change Daisy before I leave."

His mother looked up at him. "I'll do it," she said. "If you don't mind."

And that was how it began.

His mother changed the baby. His father shot a roll of film. Daisy, as usual, worked her magic on them all and the ice slowly started to thaw. There were still thirty-four years of problems left to be solved, but

Daisy discovered her grandparents and, more importantly, they discovered her.

His parents walked Hunter and Daisy out to the rental car.

"Why don't you stop back here on your way home to New York?" his father asked, clapping his son on the back. "We'd like to meet your new bride."

"We'd enjoy it, Hunter," said his mother, her blue eyes shimmering with tears. "We could give a lovely dinner party for you both to celebrate." She gave Daisy a big hug. "You're a beautiful little girl," she murmured. "As beautiful as your mommy was."

His father noisily cleared his throat. Hunter knew that old trick. Every American male who had ever been embarrassed by emotions knew that trick.

"You're doing a good job, son," he said gruffly. "Your sister would have been real happy."

Hunter shook hands with his father. He hugged his mother. Daisy accepted their kisses with a gurgling laugh. He'd taken the first step and his parents had met him halfway, something he wouldn't have believed possible a few short days ago.

"We're not going to take no for an answer, are we, Daisy?" he asked as the jet roared into the sky.

Miracles happened. The fact that he and Jeannie had met and married was proof of that.

And he couldn't help but believe there was one more miracle waiting for him on the beaches of Maui.

THE PRODUCTION shut down early Thursday afternoon when some clouds blew in from the west, making the requisite blue-sky shots impossible.

"Have fun, boys and girls," said the director, "but remember, vacation's over tomorrow morning at seven."

"The production gang's going to check out Hosegawa's General Store," Denise said to Jeannie as they gathered their gear, "and then ride out to see the Seven Sacred Pools. Why don't you come with us?"

"Thanks for the invitation," Jeannie said, "but I think I'll pass."

"We're going to have a great time," Denise urged. "Jacko said he might teach us the hula."

"As tempting as that sounds, I'm going to stick close to the hotel."

"Those baby Terminators getting you down?"

Jeannie smiled. "Either I'm getting older or they're getting tougher."

The truth was, all she wanted was a long soak in a fragrant bubble bath, dinner on the veranda, and sleep. Mindless sleep. She was tired, but work wasn't the cause. It was the endless litany of regrets.

Once back at the hotel she stopped at the front desk. "Any messages for Room 5?"

The clerk, a woman with friendly brown eyes, shook her head. "Nothing today, miss."

So what were you expecting? she thought as she ran the bathwater. She'd walked out on him without so much as leaving him a note or a telephone number.

She glanced at the clock on the nightstand. If she figured correctly, it was a little after 8:00 p.m. back home. Daisy would be sound asleep while Hunter was probably finishing supper and watching the Mets on the little TV in the kitchen.

"Call him," she said out loud. "Pick up the phone and let him know where you are. You're not in the witness protection plan."

Daisy...Burnett...the whole mess she'd left behind. She had to know.

"Hi," said a mechanical voice almost six thousand miles away. "You've reached Hunter and Jeannie Phillips. If you leave your name and number, we'll call you back as soon as we can."

Beep.

"Hunter, it's me...are you there?" She waited. Was he standing there in the hallway, glaring at the answering machine? "I'm at the White Orchid on Maui. I—what I mean is, I was wondering about Daisy and...are you there, Hunter?"

Nothing.

She placed the receiver down. A thousand possibilities, all of them dreadful, occurred to her. What if Burnett had claimed paternity and Hunter had handed Daisy over to him without even putting up a fight? What if they'd gotten into a knockdown fight and Hunter was in jail for assault and battery?

Or maybe he just didn't want to talk to her.

"This is ridiculous," she said. Hunter had made it perfectly clear that the decisions about Daisy were his to make, same as she'd chosen to keep her own counsel when it came to the family she'd lost.

She and Hunter had a wedding but they'd never quite managed to have a marriage.

And it hurt her to know that she was every bit as much to blame as he was.

THEY CALLED IT "Heavenly Hana," a place so breathtakingly beautiful that once you saw it you never wanted to leave. Gorgeous vistas, eye-popping sunsets, a Disneyland version of paradise on earth.

Hunter would have to take their word for it because as he stood beneath the banyan tree at the edge of the veranda, all he could see was his wife.

She sat with her back to him, looking out toward the ocean. Her short hair was slicked back, curling slightly at the nape as if she'd just stepped out of the shower. Everything about her was lovely: the graceful line of her shoulders, which were bared by her sapphire-blue dress, the pale apricot color of her skin in the glow of the setting sun.

She seemed so alone, yet perfectly self-contained. He'd always sensed that his wife was a woman of secrets, but never more so than at this moment. She looked so small, so incredibly fragile, yet he had the feeling there was hidden steel. She was a fighter, his Jeannie, a woman who stood up for what she believed.

He wondered if she still believed in their marriage.

He moved closer and closer, until he stood at her elbow.

"You can take my plate," she said, not looking up. "I'm finished."

"Great," he said, "but I'm not."

"Oh, God," she whispered, lowering her head. "It can't be...."

"Jeannie."

Swallowing hard, she turned around.

"I look like hell," he said. "I need a shave. I slept in these clothes. All I could think of was getting here."

His collar was open and his sleeves rolled up. He looked totally out of place in this tropical wonderland, strung-out and exhausted, and yet he was the most beautiful sight she'd ever seen.

But where was Daisy?

"You're a hard woman to find," he said.

She looked away. The intensity of his gaze was overpowering. "Something's happened," she said. "It's Daisy, isn't it?"

"Yes," he said, "it's Daisy."

She felt as if the ground were moving beneath her feet. She met his eyes. "Is Burnett her father?"

"No," said Hunter. "I am."

Hope, painful and sweet, came to life inside her heart. "I—I don't understand."

"It's really pretty simple," he said. "Burnett and Callie gave Daisy her blue eyes and dimples. I took care of the rest."

She listened as he told her the story of a man and a woman, of an attraction that should never have been. And of a baby Callie had been praying for, but one that Burnett couldn't quite believe was on its way.

"They'd been seeing each other for a month," Hunter explained. "Burnett was giving a seminar that spring in Tokyo and Callie was working as his translator."

Burnett was a married man and the father of three, part of a distinguished and highly political family. "The situation suited them both. He wasn't looking for a new family and Callie had already determined that the baby would belong to her and nobody else." Even after Callie learned that the pregnancy had put her life at risk, she was determined to see it through. "Burnett was in Caracas by then, working on a project for OPEC, but he helped Callie find the best doctors in Tokyo."

She saw the way the muscles in his cheek were working as he tried to control his emotions. "Hunter, you don't have to—"

He cleared his throat. "Burnett saw my sister the month before she delivered Daisy. I don't know why—maybe she had a premonition or something—but she told Burnett that if anything happened to her, she wanted me to raise the baby."

"And he didn't object?"

Hunter laughed ruefully. "Burnett is a practical man. He hadn't been looking to become a father again. He was relieved."

"So why did he show up at your apartment?"

"Sentiment. To give me Callie's paintings." He smiled tiredly. "To see Callie's child just once."

Jeannie's heart was racing and she placed a hand

against her chest as if to slow the rapid beating. "And that's it?"

"That's it. I stormed over to Burnett's hotel that night loaded for bear and the first thing he told me was that he had no claim on Daisy." He fixed her with a look. "You were right, Jeannie...about all of it. She's my daughter. She has been from the very start."

Jeannie's eyes burned with tears. "Better late than never, Hunter. I knew you'd come around."

"And that brings me to the next question, where do we go from here?"

She pushed back her chair and clumsily rose to her feet. She was so filled with emotion that she thought she would die of it. He stood there smack in front of her, almost daring her to walk past. Turning, she tried to dart around him, but he stepped in front of her.

"Not this time," he said. "You're not running out on me tonight." With one sudden move he tossed her over his shoulder in a fireman's carry, and started for the beach.

"Put me down, Hunter, or I'll have you arrested!"

"Go ahead," he said. "That won't stop me." He continued striding down to the beach like *Rambo in Love.*

"I'm humiliated," Jeannie said, trying to cover her face while hanging upside down. "If any of the crew sees me this way, I'm finished."

"There isn't a soul around," he said. "You're safe."

He rounded a cluster of palm trees then dumped her unceremoniously in a clump of beach grass.

Her bottom smarted like the very devil, but she refused to give him the satisfaction of letting him know.

"You were right," he said without preamble. "I used you. Everybody was right—Kate, Grantham, the whole damn bunch."

She felt as if she'd been punched in the gut. "You flew all the way to Hawaii to tell me that?"

"No. I flew here to tell you this, I love you, Jeannie."

She recoiled as if he had struck her a blow.

He pretended he hadn't noticed. Nothing was going to stop him from telling her what was in his heart. "I thought marrying you would make everything perfect. Perfect for me. Perfect for Daisy. I never asked myself if it was perfect for you." He met her gaze. "You changed our lives, Jeannie. You made that apartment into a home. But I can't figure out what you got out of the deal." All the bad jokes his colleagues had made carried with them a glimmer of truth. Jeannie had turned his life around, creating happiness where there'd been chaos.

How could he know he'd given her back her heart?

"Hunter," she began, her voice a whisper. "There's something I have to tell you...."

ONCE UPON A TIME Jeannie had had two daughters and a husband who loved her, but a fire one icy morning had changed her life forever, leaving Jeannie alone and filled with guilt that she had lived while those she loved had not.

She'd moved from Oregon to Chicago; from San Francisco to Seattle; only to end up in New York, doing the one thing she was good at: working with babies.

Hunter listened, stroking her hair as she struggled with what once was. Strange how the very thing you fear the most can sometimes give you the greatest solace. It was as if the act of telling him her story released the floodgates and the guilt she had carried around for so long began to wash away.

"Am I a substitute?" he asked, forcing her to meet his eyes again. "Is Daisy?"

"No," she whispered. "Never that." She loved Hunter and Daisy for who they were, not in memory of those she had lost.

"I love you," he said quietly. "Not what you can do for Daisy and me—you, Jeannie, and whatever you need to be happy." Those days without her had been a taste of things to come, an endless lonely string of nights without the woman he loved.

He reached for her hand, touching the gold ring on her finger. "We may have to do it all over again," he said, "just to make sure it's legal."

She hesitated, the words trapped inside her heart. She'd bared her soul and he hadn't bowed beneath the weight of her secrets.

Here it was, the commitment she had been running from every day since the fire. Another life. Another chance at happiness. *Another chance to lose every-thing...*

But wasn't that what life was about, taking chances, huge leaps of faith that sometimes led you all the way to paradise?

"I love you, Hunter," she said at last, understanding the full weight of those beautiful words. "I think we can make it work."

"I know we can."

Desire made for a wonderful beginning, but romance alone wasn't enough to make a marriage successful. It took honesty and vulnerability and compassion, and that evening on the beach at Hana they took the first step toward making their marriage work.

"All I've ever wanted is a husband and family of my own," Jeannie said. "These past four weeks have been so wonderful.... I would have done anything to make it last."

"I want you," Hunter said. "At home. At work. With a career. Without one. I don't give a damn if the house comes down around our ears and we have to hire a fleet of nannies and housekeepers to take care of things." Everything she was, was everything he needed.

The kiss they shared was one of communion, a melding of souls as well as a blending of hearts.

"Daisy," she said, finally breaking the kiss. "Where *is* she?"

Laughing, he reached for his wife's hand and helped her to her feet. "I thought you'd never ask."

He led her back to the patio where a smiling waiter sat with a sleepy Daisy on his lap.

Jeannie's happy tears spilled down her cheeks and onto the baby's golden head as she hugged Daisy tight. "We're so lucky," Jeannie said, meeting his eyes. "Luckier than I ever believed possible."

"And it's going to last a long time," Hunter said. "A lifetime."

Daisy's little face puckered in a frown and her eyes fluttered open. "Daah," she said uncertainly. Then, smiling up at Hunter: "Da-da!"

"You bet I am, Daisy," he said, drawing his wife and daughter close. "You just bet I am."

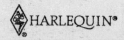

Not The Same Old Story!

 Exciting, emotionally intense romance stories that take readers around the world.

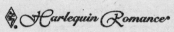 Vibrant stories of captivating women and irresistible men experiencing the magic of falling in love!

 Bold and adventurous—Temptation is strong women, bad boys, great sex!

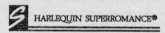 Provocative, passionate, contemporary stories that celebrate life and love.

 Romantic adventure where anything is possible and where dreams come true.

 Heart-stopping, suspenseful adventures that combine the best of romance and mystery.

LOVE & LAUGHTER Entertaining and fun, humorous and romantic—stories that capture the lighter side of love.

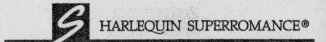

HARLEQUIN®

I N T R I G U E®

THAT'S INTRIGUE—DYNAMIC ROMANCE AT ITS BEST!

Harlequin Intrigue is now bringing you more—more men and mystery, more desire and danger. If you've been looking for thrilling tales of contemporary passion and sensuous love stories with taut, edge-of-the-seat suspense—then you'll *love* Harlequin Intrigue!

Every month, you'll meet four new heroes who are guaranteed to make your spine tingle and your pulse pound. With them you'll enter into the exciting world of Harlequin Intrigue—where your life is on the line and so is your heart!

Harlequin Intrigue—we'll leave you breathless!

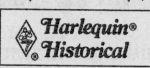

Harlequin® Historical

If you're a serious fan of historical romance,
then you're in luck!

Harlequin Historicals brings you
stories by bestselling authors, rising new stars
and talented first-timers.

Ruth Langan & Theresa Michaels
Mary McBride & Cheryl St.John
Margaret Moore & Merline Lovelace
Julie Tetel & Nina Beaumont
Susan Amarillas & Ana Seymour
Deborah Simmons & Linda Castle
Cassandra Austin & Emily French
Miranda Jarrett & Suzanne Barclay
DeLoras Scott & Laurie Grant…

You'll never run out of favorites.

Harlequin Historicals…they're too good to miss!

HH-GEN

HARLEQUIN PRESENTS®

HARLEQUIN PRESENTS
men you won't be able to resist falling in love with...

HARLEQUIN PRESENTS
women who have feelings just like your own...

HARLEQUIN PRESENTS
powerful passion in exotic international settings...

HARLEQUIN PRESENTS
intense, dramatic stories that will keep you turning
to the very last page...

HARLEQUIN PRESENTS
The world's bestselling romance series!